Unbroken

Unbroken

BY JESSIE HAAS

SCHOLASTIC INC.
New York Toronto London Auckland Sydney
Mexico City New Delhi Hong Kong

ISBN 0-439-18829-6

Published by Scholastic Inc., 555 Broadway, New York, NY 10012,
by arrangement with Greenwillow Books,
an imprint of HarperCollins Publishers.
SCHOLASTIC and associated logos are trademarks
and/or registered trademarks of Scholastic Inc.

12 11 10 9 8 7 6 5 4   7 8 9 10/0

Printed in the U.S.A.   40

First Scholastic printing, March 2001

The text of this book is set in Palatino.

FOR MICHAEL

one

Our pencils scratched steadily. Every head was bowed, but we watched Miss Spencer and Reverend Astley from under our hands or hair.

He spoke close to her ear, and the welcoming smile went stiff on her face, then vanished as she glanced our way. Behind me Luke drew a faint hissing breath. Trouble for someone.

I wondered for whom, watched my hand scrolling out an elegant line of script across the page, so regular and well formed that I barely recognized it for my own, glanced out the high window, through which the sun streamed—

"Harriet Gibson."

My pencil clattered on the floor. Miss Spencer's face, full of compassion, was turned toward me. My heart squeezed.

"Bring your things, dear," she said.

Luke's breath hissed again, and I felt her fingers touch my back. With numb hands I scrambled my books and papers into a pile and rose with them in my arms. Billy Booth gave me the pencil, with a sympathetic grimace. Then I was up the aisle, being ushered out of the room by Reverend Astley, and the thick oak door shut behind us.

"I won't keep you in suspense," he said, turning to face me the moment we were alone. "Your mother has been injured in an accident, and you must come home at once."

He took the books. His hand on my upper arm hurried me along the corridor as the clock struck the half hour. Nine-thirty in the morning—

"Is she—"

"Her condition is serious, but the doctor is hopeful." He opened the door for me. At the bottom of the stairs his buggy waited. He handed me up, climbed in himself, and turned the roan horse.

"What—what's wrong with her? What happened?"

Reverend Astley seemed to hesitate for a moment. "I don't know the details," he said finally. "An automobile was involved, and the horse took fright. Your mother was on her way back from bringing you to school, I understand."

A lump began to grow in my throat. We were late this morning. I'd jumped down over the wheel and run up the Academy steps without glancing back. Just "Bye!" over my shoulder, and the sound of Belle's hooves as Mother turned her.

Oh, please let her be all right. Please.

Barrett village blurred past, and we were out on the road, climbing between fields and pastures toward West Barrett.

Please.

"Don't look," the reverend said suddenly. "Close your eyes!"

Too late. There ahead of us was the buggy, shattered like a shot crow: broken shafts, broken axle, splintered top. It looked too fragile ever to have carried the two of us.

Farther along the sun gleamed on a motionless sorrel mound. Belle. I saw her white foot curled up toward her belly, as if ready for one last kick. The roan horse pricked his ears, and his steady trot faltered, but Reverend Astley touched him with the whip, and he clopped on.

A moment later we rounded the corner and saw West Barrett, small and high above us, just a straggling line of gray houses clinging to the hillside. Our house, smallest and grayest, leaned slightly toward the sawmill next door, as if it had gone deaf and were straining to hear what the saw was saying.

The bright moving spot behind the house was the colt, trotting back and forth. His neighs reached us even down here. Two years old, but he cried for Belle every time she left him. The sunlight suddenly glittered more brightly as my eyes filled with tears. Every morning and afternoon the hollow rang like this, and once or twice a week Mother said, "Thank goodness for that mill! At least we're not causing the only racket!"

The smell of sweat came back from the roan, and the fresh, wild scent of pine sawdust came, too, sinking down from the mill. Smoke rose from our chimney. Dr. Vesper's buggy stood in the yard. We pulled in beside it, and I leaped over the turning wheel and fell on my knees in the dirt. "Harriet!" Reverend Astley cried sharply, but I was already running up the steps.

The kitchen and sitting room were empty. I rushed through, toward the back bedroom and the sound of voices. Dr. Vesper's broad black waistcoat blocked the doorway. "Please," I said. He stepped to one side, and I stopped.

She didn't look like herself. She was as pale as the pillowcase, with a big red bruise on her forehead. Her eyes were closed, the lids bluish, and the room was very quiet.

I stepped softly toward the bed, looking at the quilt. Yes, it rose and fell. Yes, she was breathing.

After a moment she whispered, "Hello, Harry." Her eyes struggled to open. Her mouth formed a tiny curve, like a smile. "I made a mistake."

Her hands were under the quilt. I dropped to my knees beside the bed and touched her shoulder. "Oh, Mummy!"

The sound of tears was in my voice, and I heard a *tsk* from the other side of the bed. I looked up. Our neighbor Mrs. Brand sat there, in a flour-dusted apron. She shook her head. "Don't worry her."

At that Mother's eyes opened, smoothly and swiftly. She stared at the ceiling for a moment, unfocused. Then slowly her eyes turned toward me. Only her eyes. All the rest of her was still. But a faint color touched her cheeks for a second. "You don't worry me," she said clearly, and under the quilt I saw her hand move.

Mrs. Brand looked up at Dr. Vesper. Then she reached across Mother and gently drew the quilt aside.

Mother's trembling fingers stretched up. I took them in my hand, and at their touch a chill struck inward at my stomach. She shouldn't be this cold!

Her eyes closed again. Through the window came the scream of the mill saw, the scream of the colt. "Poor

Belle," Mother whispered. Then she seemed to be done talking. I didn't know if she was conscious anymore.

Behind me in the sitting room Dr. Vesper said, "No, I can't move her, not down this godforsaken hill!"

"I don't think this hill is quite God-forsaken," Reverend Astley said in a prim voice. On the other side of the bed Althea Brand stiffened and frowned.

"Oh, Judas, look at the time!" Dr. Vesper said. "I was sent for up-country!" He came in and leaned over me. His thick, wrinkled hand was beside mine, feeling Mother's pulse. Her eyelids didn't flicker.

"You'll stay, Althea, won't you?" he asked.

Mrs. Brand looked hard at him, as if trying to understand something. Then she nodded. "Yes, but I'm worried about my house. Harriet, run down quick and see if I left the kettle on. And look through and find that cat, won't you, and put her out?"

"But—" I was holding Mother's hand.

"Go on, Harry," Dr. Vesper said, giving my shoulder a squeeze. "You're young and quick. It'll just take a minute."

I couldn't say no. He was almost one of the family. But Reverend Astley could have offered! He could have let me stay. I brushed past him without excusing myself and hurried down the front steps, startling the horses.

Mrs. Brand's house was three doors down. I ran, past the windows with the white gauze curtains, past the faces. Into Mrs. Brand's house, the only other house in West Barrett with which I was familiar. We had lived here for eleven years, since I was two, and we smiled and spoke to everyone. But we were never invited past the kitchen. Althea Brand had set her back up against the other four ladies of the village and so made a point of not disapproving of us.

Of course the kettle was not on the burner, and the cat wasn't in the house either. I had scrambled through half the rooms and almost upset a lamp when I noticed her down in the little back garden, hunting. I banged out the door again and ran up the hill, feeling the drag of its steepness. Past our small field. The colt pushed against the gate, calling to me. I hurried past him and up the steps. If I got back quickly, I might hear what they were saying.

But as I came in, Dr. Vesper was laying Mother's hand back on her stomach and drawing the quilt up to her chin. "I will," he said, in a serious, reassuring voice. Turning, he drew me out to the sitting room.

"Now, Harry, I've got to go. Althea knows what to do, and I'll be back just as quick as God'll let me."

"Is she—" I couldn't finish the question. No one had told me anything. Mother and I were all each other had, and no one would tell me anything, not even Dr. Vesper, who looked hard at me for a moment, as if considering it, but who just said, "Do what Althea tells you, and help her all you can. You're a good girl, Harry. Be brave!" He chucked me under the chin and hurried out the door.

"I must leave also," Reverend Astley said, taking my hand. "I'll pray for your mother's recovery."

My hand was stiff and unresponsive in his. Could he feel how much I disliked him? "Yes," I managed to say. "Thank you."

Then the sitting room was empty, the two buggies rattled away, and I was left with Mother and Althea Brand, the screaming mill saw, and the screaming colt.

two

"Why don't you go change your clothes?" Mrs. Brand said when I came back into the room.

Mother's face was set like a mask. After a moment I saw her swallow.

"Water? Mummy, do you want a drink?"

No, her lips said soundlessly. I looked across the bed at Althea Brand. She sat straight in the hard chair, watching Mother's face with bright, steady eyes. She would do everything. It was all right to leave for a minute.

My schoolbooks were piled on the sitting-room table. Beside them was a pair of deerskin gloves that I didn't recognize—nothing special, just medium-nice gloves spattered with dark drops of something. The sun streamed across Mother's sewing machine. The dress she'd been hoping to finish by afternoon and to deliver when she picked me up from school lay as she had left it.

The clock ticked. A dying ember hissed in the kitchen stove. Slowly, making as little sound as possible, I climbed the narrow stairs to my bedroom.

It was the largest room in the house, at floor level, but the walls sloped sharply inward and ended in a strip of ceiling two feet wide. Light came in the gable ends, and the middle was shadowed. I walked over to look out the south window.

I was above the swallows here. I could look down on their backs. The land fell away sharply behind the houses, fifteen feet down to a narrow shelf of flat land, and then down again to the river. "If you ever get to the big city," Mother said to me once, "you won't feel like a rube. You've already lived in a skyscraper!"

I turned from the window and sat to unlace my boots. My fingers were shaking. I crushed them together in my lap and folded my body over them.

Don't cry. Don't. Crying makes it real. I clenched my teeth and threw my head back. "Don't let it know you're afraid," Mother always said of growling dogs and high-strung horses. I hugged myself hard, straining every muscle to a feeling of strength. But when I bent to the bootlaces again, my fingers still shook.

I slipped out of my school skirt and blouse and into the new calico dress Mother had just made me. We liked brighter calico than the West Barrett ladies. It was one more thing against us.

I started down the stairs, and halfway my feet just stopped. Pebbly silver wallpaper with green flecks, light above in the bedroom and light below in the kitchen, and I was suspended between, like a moth in a spider's web. I didn't know how I felt or how I was supposed to feel. Hope, or fierce prayer, or despair: if I chose one, I was settling things, and I didn't know how things really stood. Mother would have told me with one swift glance, but Mother's eyes were closed.

When they don't tell you, it's usually bad.

I found I was hugging myself again, leaning stiffly forward. Stop. Down one step, down the next, and into the kitchen, which smelled of warm tomato plants. The kitchen, with its geraniums and seedlings in the windows, its bright mats and the green china teapot, was Mother. The whole house was Mother, and it seemed to embrace me. I drew an easier breath and walked through the sitting room to her bedside.

There we sat through the morning. Mother's face looked troubled sometimes. A frown came between her brows and gradually smoothed away. But she never opened her eyes, and she never spoke.

The mill saw stopped. Noon. In the greater silence I could hear my stomach growl. Mrs. Brand must be hungry, too. "Would you like bread and jam? And tea?"

She nodded, and I went away to fix lunch. I was hungry, but when I took the first bite of bread, spread with blackberry jam we made last fall, I couldn't seem to chew it. I forced it down in a dry lump that hurt my throat and followed it with a swallow of too-hot tea. Althea Brand ate her slice of bread and drank her tea, never turning her gaze from Mother's face.

The saw started up. The sound seemed to waken the colt's despair. He screamed again and again. There was no sign that his cries disturbed Mother. Her eyelids didn't flicker. But over the next two hours Althea Brand began to jerk in her chair at every neigh.

"Can you shut him up somehow?"

I couldn't. He wanted Belle, who lay dead beside the road. Would someone bury her, or would she be dragged away to rot in the back corner of a field? Pretty Belle. Without even closing my eyes I could see the exact outline of the white snip on her nose, how at its edges the white seemed to overlap the chestnut of her face like a smear of paint.

Mother drew a deep, long breath. We looked. A long pause followed, and then another breath came.

Althea Brand's eyes seemed to grow and darken. Her mouth got smaller. She stared intently into Mother's face. Then she reached across the bed and twitched the quilt back. "Take her hand!"

She pushed back the quilt on her own side, took Mother's other hand, and leaned forward so their faces were close. "Ellen!" she said sharply. "Ellen! You hold on now! You think of this child!"

Mother's hand was freezing, and the cold seemed to spread up my arm into my chest and throat. I couldn't speak.

Mrs. Brand leaned closer. "Ellen, don't you give in! What will become of Harriet if you give in like this?"

The slow, deep breaths went on, with terrible pauses between. Mrs. Brand began to chafe the back of Mother's hand, so hard it made a rasping sound. "*Harriet!* Say something! Call her back!"

I opened my mouth, but only a whimper came out. "Muh!"

Mother's eyes opened, in the swift way she had whenever I was threatened. She was *there*. Her eyes glowed in her white mask of a face, and she turned and smiled at me tenderly. I felt tears on my cheeks.

Then she bit her lip and shook her head slightly, still smiling. "I can't." Just a whisper. "You'll be fine, Harry. I know."

"Mummy."

Very near the house and as loudly as he could, the colt neighed, as if trying to slam his voice into Belle and force her back to him.

"Be careful," Mother whispered. "And—" She paused, smiled and grimaced, as if at some small, amusing impediment, and shook her head again. "Andy will tell you— Yes, I'm coming!" She seemed to answer the colt. "Just a minute. Harry—" Her hand tightened slightly on mine. "Love . . . yes," she whispered. "Yes."

She smiled past me; her breath sighed out; the clock in the sitting room ticked, ticked. A longer pause, but the next breath would come. There! Trembling. Wasn't it?

Althea Brand's hand reached to Mother's face, tenderly touched her eyelids, and smoothed them shut. The breath was hers. She was crying.

I looked across at her, and she shook her head at me. "Harriet. Harriet."

My face seemed to be smiling. I didn't know what to do about it.

"You'll want to be alone with her." Mrs. Brand went past the end of the bed, fumbling in her sleeve for her handkerchief. I heard her in the kitchen, blowing her nose.

Mother lay smiling on the pillow, a little color in her cheeks. She looked as she had this morning. I would just bend over and whisper in her ear, and she'd wake up.

I bent, and something seemed to catch me, as if a sharp, hot stake had been driven through my body. Don't do that. Don't. Stay here, hold her hand, see her smile in the sunlight, while the sweet scent of mock orange hangs in the air.

I remember that Dr. Vesper came back at some point and led me from the room, made me drink some blackberry cordial.

I remember I was cold. Very cold. Not even Mother's thick wool shawl could warm me.

I remember them talking. They said Althea Brand would take me to her house. But when she wanted to, I shook my head. I couldn't really see anything. I didn't look at her. I shook my head, and they didn't make me.

"—lay her out in?" They wanted me to choose a dress. Her pretty green print. That was her favorite dress. Did I tell them that? The colt screamed and screamed, and Dr. Vesper said, "Somebody should shoot that son of a bitch!"

I could see him for a moment. He stood at the sitting-room window. He was crying. "No," I said.

"No," he said. "Oh, damn it all, Harry."

I didn't cry until I went upstairs, and I was alone, and I would always be alone. I used to feel a strong line from Mother's heart to mine whenever I saw her, and love moved along it like a telegraph signal. Now the line was cut.

I cried quietly until I couldn't be quiet anymore, and then I cried out loud. Mrs. Brand came up and rubbed my back for a while and went away again.

Dark came. I would never sleep again. My eyes were open, and the dark pressed against them.

She was driving out of our dooryard. I could see the white-washed rocks and the pansies. She was driving Belle.

I stood up. "But you're dead!"

Belle stopped, and Mother reached down to me. I took her hand, and she squeezed mine. We looked into each other's faces. The sun shone around us, and I could feel the line, I could feel the love. Some of Mother's side hair was loose, and the sun caught the tendrils.

Belle stamped. Mother smiled, drew her hand away, and shook the reins over Belle's back. I turned and watched them go down the hill. My heart was light and free and happy.

My eyes opened against the dark. Happy. I didn't think I would ever feel happy again.

They *are* dead.

But they're all right. She was letting me know. She was telling me. It was clearer than a dream, and realer than a dream, because I knew all the time that they were dead. I *said* they were dead. It wasn't just a wish because if I'd had my wish, she wouldn't have driven away.

I wanted to get up and tell someone. They came. They're all right.

Outside in the dark all was quiet. No neighing. Maybe the colt had seen them, too.

three

I awoke in sunshine. Swallows dived past the window, and the mill saw was singing.

I sat up under the sloped ceiling, with a heavy head and aching eyes. A stripe of cold ran down my back. My arms and legs had a cringing feel to them, as if they wanted to curl up tight.

But my heart felt clear and as open as the window. I could see her so precisely, in her bright calico dress just like the one I wore now. I could feel the press of her hand. It was real, not a dream. She had come back to tell me she was all right.

The shawl was still wound around me. I unwrapped it and walked to the window. Far below, the colt grazed intently, as if making up for lost time—snatch snatch snatch. The sunlight made a streak over his round back, sliding as he moved. Below him the willow branches stirred, the little river sparkled and splashed.

Mother loved this view. She must be out there somewhere, folded invisibly into the air.

I turned, spreading my arms as if to catch something. Nothing stopped them, though, and the sunlight dazzled my eyes. I was desperately thirsty. A cup of tea . . .

When I came down to the kitchen, Dr. Vesper sat at the table. For a second my mind seemed to disconnect. Was she better? Was she only sick now, not dead?

He looked up wearily. "Morning, Harry. Tea?" The pot stood on the table. There was the smell of biscuits on the air and a plate with crumbs and jam in front of him.

I sat down. He poured out tea for me, then got up to take the biscuits out of the warming oven. He was making a guest of me in my own home. Around the happy freedom in my heart something seemed to tighten.

"Althy went home for a minute," Dr. Vesper said. His voice seemed deeper than usual, rasping and slow. It was made that way by sorrow. I wanted to tell him, "I saw Mother last night."

But he went on. "I need to tell you some things, Harry, and I have to be quick. Somebody needs me."

I sipped the tea. Too strong. We like it light, so the perfume comes through, and not the bitterness. This tea seemed to bite the back of my mouth.

"I'm the executor of your mother's estate," Dr. Vesper said. "You need to know how things are left, Harry."

How things are left? I could think only of the closed door beyond the sitting room, the dimness and stillness that seemed to spread from there.

"You're to go to your aunt Sarah," he said.

"*What?*" Aunt Sarah hated us. She was my father's sister, and I'd seen her only a few times in my life.

"It's what your mother wanted. She said it to me, and she set it down in her will. 'Sarah's ways aren't my ways,' she said to me, 'but she'll be good to Walter's child.' "

"*When?* When did she say that? She didn't say it to

15

me!'' How could she not have said it to me? How could she have wasted precious moments of breath on *them*—Mrs. Brand, Dr. Vesper—while I was sent away?

Dr. Vesper looked straight at me. His eyes were bloodshot and red around the rims. "There's no reason not to tell you now," he said. "Your mother never expected to live to see you grown."

Around my head the air seemed to hum. "Why?"

"She had a bad heart, Harry. She didn't have much time left." He stopped abruptly and looked down.

"But why—" I couldn't even whisper. My throat squeezed shut.

"Your mother was . . ." His voice went down too deep. He paused and took a breath. "She said to me, 'Harry and I are going to be happy while we can. When we have to be sad, we'll be darned good and sad, but right now we'll be happy.' But she made her plans, too, and you're to go to Sarah."

"I can't stay here?"

He didn't hear it as a question. "That's all right," he said in a reassuring voice. "The house will have to be sold anyway. I'll take care of that, and pay the debts, and anything left I'll put in the bank for you."

Sold? Our house? But she was *here.* This was where I saw her, driving past our white rocks. *Here.*

"Can you write Sarah a note, Harry?" Dr. Vesper was asking. "I'll stop by the farm this morning and tell her everything, but a little something from you might help things along."

I stood up numbly and walked to Mother's desk in the sitting room. With my back to the bedroom door, I took out the paper, opened the ink bottle, and wrote:

May 27, 1910
West Barrett, Vermont

Dear Aunt Sarah,
Mother died about four o'clock yesterday
afternoon. She left me to you.
Dr. Vesper will bring this letter and explain.
          Your—

Your what? The pen stopped, making a blot. Your . . .

          Your affectionate Niece,
          Harriet Gibson

Dr. Vesper came in behind me. I folded the note and
gave it to him.

"Harry," he said, stopped, and cleared his throat.
"Harry, just so you know, I'm named in the will if something happens. Sarah isn't the only one you have. I'm
named, too."

Then the kitchen door opened. Mrs. Brand was back,
and Dr. Vesper, with a harried glance at the clock,
departed.

"Do you want to sit with her?" Mrs. Brand asked.

Sit with her? Oh. Go in and sit beside her body. "No."
I closed my eyes. "No. I . . . have to go back upstairs."

"Did you eat anything? Have some tea."

I shook my head and went past her. My heart felt
swollen and heavy, and my head was heavy, and my
throat had closed tight.

In my room I stood still. The sunlight reached toward
me across the bare floor. Through the screen I could hear
the swallows chortle to one another.

A bad heart?

Sold?

The air seemed thick, impossible to push through.

Debts? What debts did we have?

We. I always said "we." *We* always said "we," but part of her was *I*, and grown up, and keeping secrets. Debts, and a bad heart.

But she sent me to the Academy. How did she pay for that?

She drove me there and back every day.

She didn't have much time left.

My thick, heavy feet moved me toward the window. The bright grass. The sparkling river. The willows tossing and the swallows diving for flies . . .

It will have to be sold.

Mother and I made our own little world. What I wished and what I thought, my talents and my grades at school, mattered more to her than anything.

Without her I was no one. I must do what her words on a piece of paper told me. I must do whatever any adult told me. I couldn't even stay here, in the world we had made together. The house was her, the house was us, and it would have to be sold.

My hands seemed to rise by themselves, independent of my arms or will. My wrists felt numb and tingled, but above them, disconnected, my hands were strong. My fingers spread wide and pushed slowly into the screen, each fingertip making a separate indentation. With a *pop* and a *scritch* the thin, rusted wires began to separate and then to break.

I looked down on the bottle blue backs of the swallows.

Down, down, on the bright green grass. Down, to the bottom of my skyscraper.

Folded invisibly into the air.

The saw blade paused for breath, and in the little silence I heard hoofbeats. My fingers jumped back, and broken wire stabbed them.

Up from the river the colt came galloping. His head was high, his nostrils wide, his ears flat back. He swept in a wide loop around the pasture, then stopped at the very edge where the land dropped down to the river and gazed out over the tops of the willows.

Playing. All by himself.

His head turned. He looked toward the pasture gate, thinking of his mother. He was just her color, bright chestnut. Beautiful. "Keeping a horse just to drive that girl to school is bad enough," the West Barrett ladies used to say, "but a useless colt into the bargain?" When I overheard that, I told Mother, and we laughed.

"Harry and I are going to be happy...."

Tears were running down my face. "I just wanted to *ask* you," I said, into the glittering, empty air.

No answer came. She wasn't ever going to answer my questions again, and I was stuck here. I had been going to jump, and now I wouldn't, because of the bright running colt, and my fingers were stuck in the screen. The broken wires stabbed into them like porcupine quills.

A tearing sob burst out of me, another, another. The colt stared up at the high window, and shied, and ran. And up the stairs two at a time came Althea Brand. She burst into the room and cried, "Oh, good Lord in heaven!"

I looked over my shoulder to see her standing back a little, one hand up to her mouth.

"I'm *stuck!*"

She looked behind her and then came forward slowly, as if I were dangerous. I felt my hot face streaming with tears, my hot, throbbing fingers, but inside, a cold little shock. This is too much. This is more than she can do.

The tears stopped coming, all by themselves. I sniffed hard and saw her wince.

"I'm sorry. Could—could you wipe my face?"

She came closer, fishing in her sleeve, then drew out a dampish handkerchief and mopped my eyes and nose. When that was done, she looked at my hands, and her normal expression of practical competence began to reappear. "Will the sewing shears cut that screen, do you think?"

"I think so."

"Then—" She started to turn, then stopped and looked hard at me. I looked back at her, knowing I must not be a reassuring sight. But I felt a hardness inside that was like her hardness, stiffening me all up the center.

"I will not jump out the window," I said.

She nodded once, as if that settled that, and went away.

I pushed my fingers forward to keep the screen from stabbing deeper. I watched the colt graze, listened to Althea's quick steps downstairs, feeling straight and quiet, suspended between one state and another.

You will have to be careful.

The thought presented itself that way, as if somone else were speaking. I belonged to no one. I must not ask too much and drive my friends away.

Althea snipped the screen away from my fingers and

picked out the rusty, embedded fragments. "Come downstairs," she said, looking at the ten splayed rips in the screen as if the destruction pained her. I looked back at them as I followed her, ten spots of brightness, where the sky and willow branches showed through clearly.

She sat me at the kitchen table, pumped a basin of cold water, and made me soak my fingers. "You stay put!" she said, darted down the road to her own house, and came back with an old pair of cotton gloves and a tin of ointment. She dried my fingers on a clean towel and began spreading the yellow, strong-smelling stuff over the cuts. On her left hand her two gold rings clicked together. The wide ring on her middle finger was grooved by the other, narrower one, which had rubbed against it for years.

"The wide one was her husband's ring," Mother told me once. "She's worn it since he died."

He died. Everyone must have died on Althea Brand, because she was alone, and she'd been alone as long as I had known her. Once, or twice, or many times she must have felt the way I did now.

I looked up at her face. It was paler than yesterday, holding something back. Maybe she was trying not to remember this feeling, or maybe it was always with her. Did it ever go away? Did you ever feel better? If you did feel better, maybe you hated yourself for that.

But I saw Mother. Last night I saw her.

Althea's yellowish old ear was near my face. Barely above a whisper I said, "I dreamed about her last night."

Althea looked up. Tears brimmed in her eyes, but a brilliant, wavering smile lit her face. "*Did* you? Then she's all right!"

I couldn't speak. I could only look.

"They come back to comfort us. That's what I believe."

"I woke up. I was so happy—" I clamped down to keep from crying.

"But you weren't fooled, were you? You *knew* she was gone. But she's all right. We can't understand it, but they *are* all right!"

Althea's face made me cry, she looked so happy, so reassured. As my tears started, she reached forward and gathered me into a hug, the first time ever. "You'll be all right, too, Harriet. I *promise!*"

I still couldn't eat. I made tea, our way, and sipped that.

"You've got to get something down you," Althea said. "I'll beg some milk from Julia Gould and make you a cornstarch pudding."

I shook my head. "She won't—"

"Oh, yes, she will!" Althea said. "She's dying for the news. She won't get it from me, but she won't care to miss the chance."

"*I* don't even know. What happened?"

Althea's eyes dimmed. "I don't rightly know, Harriet. A Model T came down this road, and I'd no more than watched it out of sight when back it came, and the reverend driving lickety-split behind it. Before I could get over here, the Model T man was off again after the doctor. Don't even know who he was."

"He left his gloves. On the sitting-room table."

"Andy Vesper will know," Althea said. "Now, this may take a few minutes. Will you be all right by yourself?"

She looked at me kindly. She thought I should go sit with Mother.

"I'll go check on the colt," I said.

The sun was high and warm on my head as I walked down the road, past the white rocks, through the heavy stream of scent from the mock orange bush. Those creamy four-cornered blossoms were Mother's favorite flower.

The colt came to the barway when he saw me there. He sniffed my pockets and hands. The lanolin smell beneath the gloves made him flip his lip in the air.

Then he sighed, looking off over my shoulder with a troubled expression. His muzzle pressed heavily into my palm. I could feel the teeth behind the velvet. His ears pricked toward the road, drooped back, and again twitched forward. His hope made tears run out of my eyes. More tears. I was so tired of crying.

I rested my forehead on his neck, feeling his animal warmth and the heat of the sun on his coat. He was all I had left.

My head came up so suddenly that the colt shied. *Did* I have him? Or was he among the possessions Dr. Vesper expected to sell?

I looked up at the house. It was full of our things— books, dishes, dresses and boots, and uncounted odds and ends. Was any of it mine?

I looked the colt over. He was in an awkward phase, front and back halves growing at different rates. But he would be a good Morgan. The men who kept trying to buy him proved that.

"A horse is not an extravagance," Mother always said. "Without that mare I doubt you'd get an education."

Two horses *were* an extravagance, but we couldn't bear

to part with him, and we were two people. "Someday we'll go our separate ways," Mother said, "or you can train him and sell him to pay for your college."

Now he was untrained. He couldn't take me anywhere, and he wouldn't bring in much money.

And if he wouldn't bring in much money, perhaps I would be allowed to keep him.

With stinging fingers, I broke off a branch of mock orange and carried it into the house. Althea Brand turned from the stove and made as if to move her pudding off the burner.

"No. I'll go in by myself."

The sitting room was quiet. Sunlight streamed in the window, and the sewing machine, silhouetted against it, looked like an animal grazing on the folds of fabric. Who would finish that dress? Was that one of our debts? *My* debts now.

I stood with my hand on the back of her chair. Here she sat every day, between my going to school and my returning. The pine-scented breeze coming through the screen was the air she used to breathe, while she bent over the fabric and pulled it through the machine, while her feet steadily rocked the treadle.

When I was little, I played beneath the machine or just sat there, tracing the iron lacework of legs and treadle with my fingers. Once a week I dusted the carved oak flowers and ribbons on the drawers. The sewing machine was our grandest piece of furniture and our most essential. Mother went to it late at night sometimes, saying, "I'm going to print us some money, Harry!" Sometimes I would go to sleep to the rock and thump of the treadle and that cough she got when she worked too hard.

If she had died of that cough, I would want to break up the sewing machine with an ax. I would want to kill myself, for my blindness and childishness.

But she didn't. I'll keep the sewing machine, I decided. She made our living with it. I should be able to make a living, too.

With that thought uppermost, I pushed open the bedroom door.

The hush stopped me. I could almost feel it on my face. Mother lay with her hands folded across the front of her green dress. Her face on the pillow looked like a wax carving, and not a good likeness either. The distant, reserved expression was all wrong.

I was surprised at how cool I felt. This wasn't Mother. This was what she'd left behind.

Her hands were like herself, though. There was the burn she got cooking last winter. Her wedding ring hung loosely on her finger. That hand was the one she'd reached to me last night. I remembered feeling the ring.

I stretched my eyes wide against the smarting tears. Maybe she would come again tonight. If she didn't, that must be the last touch I remembered. I slid the branch between her hands, keeping it flexed so my fingers didn't even brush her dress. Then I laid my head beside hers on the pillow.

"Good night, Mother," I heard myself whisper. I went out to the kitchen before I could think about that.

Althea Brand stood at the stove, stirring briskly, while tears ran down her face. I didn't want to cry anymore. I stood back, hugging myself, and she didn't know I was there.

But when her tears began to drip and hiss on the stove

top, it made me laugh. Then I couldn't help crying. We hugged each other, and that was still so strange it brought us around quickly. We spooned down warm cornstarch pudding and drank tea and waited for the doctor.

He came late in the afternoon, looking exhausted and in a hurry, sat down at the kitchen table, and handed me a folded piece of paper. "I'll leave you two to talk," Althea Brand said, slipping out the door.

I read.

> Dear Harriet,
> Of course you will have a home with us for as long as you need one.
> We will be down to the funeral. Please have your things ready as we must get back to milk.
> I am very sorry.
> Sincerely,
> Sarah Hall

Dr. Vesper was looking skeptically at the cup of black tea Althea Brand had left him. Without raising his eyes, he asked, "What kind of letter did she send you, Harry?"

I gave it to him. He glanced over it, and his eyebrows jumped. "Well," he said, "guess that's all right then."

What in the letter had surprised him? What had Aunt Sarah said when he gave her the news? I didn't dare ask. I couldn't afford to hear anything that might make me hate her.

Instead I said, "I have to ask you some things."

At that moment he noticed my gloved hands. I looked down at them. The ointment had soaked through in dark, greasy patches.

He doesn't tell *me* everything, I thought, and folded my hands in my lap.

"What do you want to know, Harry?"

"Will you tell me what happened?"

He looked down again at his tea. "The horse bolted, and the buggy smashed, and . . . Sam came down from the mill and shot the mare. She had a broken leg."

"Mother said—she told me she'd made a mistake."

"I believe she did. It was John Gale in the car, big farmer from upriver. He said she tried to keep the mare on the road instead of turning off. He was coming down that hill standing on all three pedals, and he said to me, 'I could see her get her dander up, and she took hold of those reins,' and of course the jeestly thing backfired. If she'd just turned off . . . there was an open gate right there, she could have. . . ." His voice had been deepening, and now it squeezed off.

"He left his gloves," I said.

"John Gale? He's a good man, Harry. You'll see him tomorrow, I expect." He paused and cleared his throat. "The reverend been next or nigh you?"

"Not yet."

"He will be." Dr. Vesper took a wincing sip of tea. "Be civil, Harry."

My heart swelled, and my eyes prickled. It was so moving to be understood. I had to wait a moment before I could ask, "What did you mean, that you're named in her will?"

"I'm your mother's executor, and I'm partway your guardian. I'll be looking out for you."

"But—" My heart beat harder, but I made myself ask. "But I can't stay with you?"

He hesitated, glancing at me under his heavy brows. My stomach sank. Careful, I thought. Careful. Don't ask too much.

"You could for all of me, Harry," he said, "and the Old Lady agrees." The Old Lady was Mrs. Vesper. "But you do have family, and . . . there's lots of reasons to go to them. Your mother thought so. That's what she wrote in her will, and it's what she asked me to do on—yesterday."

"Oh. Then . . . what are the debts? Who do we owe money to? You can tell me," I said as he seemed to retreat. "I'm not a baby."

"That's right, Harry. I'll give you that." He thought a moment. "I don't know the money amounts, but I believe it's the store in Barrett you owe, mostly, that and the Academy. And I should think the sale of the house would cover that. You'll come out free and clear and with a little bit left over."

"And when you sell the house—"

Dr. Vesper raised his head and looked straight across the table at me. "Yes?"

"What can I keep?"

He didn't answer right away. I could hear the hush. Did he think I was heartless, asking about *things* the day after my mother's death? *Was* I heartless?

"Harry," he said at last, "you've been thinking. What do you want to keep?"

"The sewing machine," I said. "The colt."

His eyes widened. He sat staring at me for a moment, and then he started to smile, sadly and wearily, but with a true sparkle in his eye. "Poor Sarah!" he said. "At most she'll expect you to bring a couple of carpetbags. I can't wait to see her face when you turn up with a big old sewing machine and an unbroken colt!"

Althea came back, and Reverend Astley arrived. How was I expecting to get my effects up to Sarah's farm, and did I really want the colt? And a sewing machine? A dress for the funeral, the time for the funeral, when the coffin was arriving, and how I would get down to Barrett. "And really, child, what *are* you going to do with that animal?"

The voices went on. My throat hurt, and my head ached. I felt as if I were thinning out somehow, getting ready to disappear.

Suddenly Dr. Vesper snapped his fingers. "Hey! John Gale was asking was there anything he could do for you. He'll bring your things up to Sarah's, and the colt, too, I should think."

That seemed to settle things. Soon the two men went away, and Althea and I were left alone. I was so tired I could hardly see her; she was just a blur across the kitchen table.

"We'll have some more tea," she said to me, "and then we'd better start packing."

four

"*Walter Gibson, 1873–1899. Ellen Gibson, 1877–*"
Their names on the headstone steadied me. I stared at them, straining my eyes wide. I was alone now. Completely alone. She didn't come last night. Time was passing and carrying me away from her.

Many people had come to the graveside service. I couldn't look at them. Reverend Astley's words came through from time to time, though I tried not to listen.

"He maketh me to lie down in green pastures . . ."

I didn't want to cry. She was all right. She'd come back once to tell me. But though I clenched my teeth and squeezed my eyes shut, tears poured down my face. I had to strain my muscles tight to keep from sobbing aloud.

Someone nudged my arm. A handkerchief was offered. I wiped my face and blew my nose. An aura of lye soap clung to the handkerchief, which belonged to Aunt Sarah. I held it to my nose, sniffing, and the sharp scent revived me.

"Thou preparest a table before me in the presence of mine enemies . . ."

I looked at the people now; it seemed to dry my eyes.

Aunt Sarah, beside me, was as solid as a sofa set upright, covered in straining black broadcloth. Her face was just as I remembered, heavy jawed, with big, rather staring eyes. She looked sober, but not tearful.

"Surely goodness and mercy . . ."

Next to her Uncle Clayton seemed small and loose in his clothes. Aunt Sarah had been born fourteen years before my father. Clayton was old enough to be my grandfather.

". . . house of the Lord forever."

Across from me Dr. Vesper stared into the grave with tears running down his face. I looked quickly at Mrs. Vesper—the Old Lady—who had one arm linked through his and her face hidden in a handkerchief. Althea Brand looked grim, and the four ladies behind her looked grimmer: the four ladies of West Barrett, who had come down the hill together, courtesy of a rented wagon from the sawmill.

Some of the millmen were there, too. I saw Frank Watts, who had taken Mother walking a few times, and Earl Cooney, who once got drunk and serenaded my window in error. There were quite a few of Mother's customers, wearing dresses she had made. Miss Spencer hadn't come. She'd be in class now, teaching Latin. But Luke was there. Shaken with crying, she stood very close to her mother. While I watched, Mrs. Mitchell put an arm around her. I looked away.

Now here was a man I didn't know, clean shaven, squeezing his hatbrim in his hands and looking soberly at the ground. That would be John Gale, who had driven the Model T. And next to him—

My stomach jumped. Did I know this man? I seemed to remember him—he seemed to look exactly like himself—

31

but who was he? He was thin and bent, and he must have had stomach trouble because he kept one arm pressed across his front—

No, he didn't *have* an arm, not a whole arm. His sleeve was pinned up, and what I'd thought was his forearm was just a large crease in his coat. He had a thin white beard, stained yellow around the mouth, and pale eyes that didn't stay fixed like everyone else's. Instead he looked around the cemetery, with a pleased expression that made me look, too, at the green grass and flowering mock orange and spiraea. There was nothing unseemly in his attitude. When he glanced at the coffin, he seemed almost grateful, as if for an invitation to some pleasant occasion.

It *is* pleasant, I thought. The sky was blue, the sun warm, and it warmed the grass until it gave off its green smell. I hadn't been able to forgive that this morning.

But Mother was all right. I remembered now how she'd reached her hand down from the buggy with a reassuring smile, while Belle stamped and snorted.

This day was always going to come. She had a bad heart, and she knew she wouldn't live to see me grown—and she was all right. The man with the stained beard seemed to know that. The free way he held up his head and glanced around at the day, and respectfully at the coffin, told me that. Who was he? In spite of his thin, rusty, impoverished look, he was the most interesting person there.

Unexpectedly it was over. I'd missed the words I dreaded most: the earth, ashes, dust. People were coming toward me now. I held myself straight and clenched my fingers around Aunt Sarah's wet handkerchief.

First to approach was John Gale. He was pale, his skin furrowed like snow that's been rained on. His sad eyes met mine directly as he took my hand between his two warm ones.

"Miss Gibson? I'm as sorry as I can be," he said.

I couldn't answer. All I could do was nod.

"The doctor says I'm to transport your things—"

Aunt Sarah stirred. "That won't be necessary. Her uncle and I will bring her things up with us in the buggy."

John Gale gave my hand a strong squeeze and released it, turning to face Aunt Sarah. "Ma'am, I'm John Gale, and I caused the accident that took her mother's life. I'd like to help."

Aunt Sarah seemed to swell on a long, indrawn breath. Two spots of color burned on her cheeks, and her eyes flashed. "I thank you," she said firmly, "but no help is needed."

John Gale pressed his lips together and glanced at me. He seemed full of courage still but unsure what to say next.

I couldn't help him. On her other side Uncle Clayton seemed to shrivel inside his clothes, and I wanted to shrivel, too. How could Dr. Vesper have let me keep the colt and the sewing machine? Didn't he know that was too much?

I looked for him but felt him first, a big, warm hand on my shoulder. "Hello, Sarah," he said. Then the other hand was on my other shoulder, and he was like a wall at my back. "You'll have a more comfortable ride up— has John been telling you? He'll bring Harry's things."

Aunt Sarah's whole face was red now, and her eyes were as hard as marbles. She looked from one man to

33

another, and I was glad to be short and beneath her gaze. "I just don't see the need," she said.

"Well now, Sarah, Harry's bringing her whole inheritance with her." His hands gave me a squeeze, so small it must have been invisible. "It don't amount to much, but it's what she's got: three big carpetbags, as I understand, and a Singer sewing machine, and a two-year-old colt."

Aunt Sarah's chin worked visibly, and her eyes fixed on mine. I felt my knees start to weaken. I straightened them and hoped they would lock.

"Blame me if you like, Sarah," Dr. Vesper said, and her eyes lifted swiftly. She *did* like. "But Harry's made some good choices. Good Morgan that'll get her somewhere someday, good sewing machine that her mother made a living with—"

Aunt Sarah sniffed. The sniff was directed at Mother, and I wanted to strike, right in the middle of the broadcloth waist. But Dr. Vesper's hands were heavy on my shoulders, and from Aunt Sarah's shadow Uncle Clayton said timidly, "Put the hoss in the pasture with the rest of the stock. No trouble, really."

Aunt Sarah looked down at me. I stared back at her, my cheeks and eyes burning. Her face changed in some way that I didn't understand. She turned to John Gale.

"Mr. Gale, it appears your help will be most welcome. You may follow us up to West Barrett."

She turned to go. I was expected to follow, but I couldn't move. I was shaking all over, ready to fall.

"*Andrew!*" I was hugged deep into a lilac-scented bosom. The Old Lady. "You can't allow this!"

"It's what Ellen wanted. They owe it to her to try, Sarah and Harry both."

"It's too much!" Mrs. Vesper said, wrapping her arms tighter around me and dropping tears onto my head.

I cried, too—shook all over with it, helpless. Oh, *Mother*. Did I really? Did I *owe* it to her to live with this horrible woman who despised us both?

Aunt Sarah would be climbing into the buggy. She'd be watching me with her marble blue eyes.

I drew back from Mrs. Vesper and used the lye-scented handkerchief. Dimly I heard her say, "No, Andy, I *won't* hush! Harriet, you've got a home with us if you need one. You remember that!"

Then Dr. Vesper drew my arm through his and led me toward the buggy. The four ladies of West Barrett were clustered at the wheel. Luke stood almost in our path. To my swimming eyes she appeared to waver like a reflection on the water. "Harry?"

No more hugs. Please. No more crying.

She hung back for a moment. Then she darted forward and gripped my hand hard. She was sobbing, but she managed to ask, "Will you come back to school?"

"I don't know."

She squeezed my hand again. Then she was gone, and Dr. Vesper was helping me up into the buggy, where I squashed in beside Aunt Sarah.

Uncle Clayton turned the white horse, and it jogged heavily up the street. Aunt Sarah was a hot bulk beside me. On the other side the strut of the buggy top dug into my shoulder. The breeze dried my face. I closed my eyes.

I could tell when we reached the edge of town by the

roughness of the road, the shade, the tilt backward as the horse began to climb. Every day I'd made this ride, beside Mother, behind Belle. . . .

I kept my eyes closed as long as I could, wanting not to see the place where the grass was crushed beside the road from Belle's body being dragged away, the fragment of buggy hood that no one had picked up.

But my eyes opened too early. I turned to look at the people beside me. Aunt Sarah gazed straight ahead, lips pressed tightly together. Uncle Clayton just drove, looking around him curiously. I saw by his face when we passed the spot. His head turned until his eyes met mine. He jumped and looked straight ahead again. "Clayton is harmless," Mother always said. I closed my eyes again and listened for the sound of John Gale's team and wagon behind us.

When I walked into the house, my footsteps sounded hollow. The house was not much emptier—three carpetbags beside the door, the sewing machine folded down into its table—but it sounded empty.

I was alone for the moment. Outside Aunt Sarah directed John Gale and Uncle Clayton, horses tramped, and wagon wheels rumbled. Inside, it was still. Already it felt like someone else's house.

I climbed the stairs. On the bare mattress lay my calico work dress. A rectangle of sunlight reached along the floor. After a moment's hesitation I crossed to the skyscraper window. At sight of the long drop my stomach seemed to fall through my body. I braced my hand on the window frame. My fingers throbbed inside my black gloves.

Would I ever again be high enough to look down on a swallow's back?

The willows shifted above the bright water. The little river made its rushing sound, the saw sang, and right in front of my nose a mosquito climbed through one of the holes in the screen.

"Come on in," I whispered.

"Harriet?" Aunt Sarah called from the bottom of the stairs. "Harriet, where are you?"

I will hate my name, I thought. She'll make me hate my own name.

I went to the stairs and looked down to meet her eyes. Instantly I felt myself stiffen, the way a dog stiffens and bristles at a strange dog's challenge. "I'll *be* right *down*."

Aunt Sarah's form seemed to broaden and fill the stairwell. Her eyes took on a glassy hardness. Without a word she turned away.

I sat on the bare bed, shaking. I don't fight. Though Lucretia and I call ourselves Luke and Harry, though we ride horses and climb trees, we aren't rough girls. I like people who like me, and before this I paid no attention to anyone who didn't.

But already I had made Aunt Sarah angry.

"Well, she started it," I whispered to the still room. "She started it."

I changed my dress. When I came downstairs, the carpetbags were no longer beside the door. John Gale and Uncle Clayton were carrying out the sewing machine, and Aunt Sarah stood in the kitchen, looking around and tapping her foot.

I looked where she was looking, at the tomato seedlings in the window, the pots and pans on their hooks, the teapot and the cups. Last night, packing, Althea and I had not known what I could take. If we removed anything but Mother's and my personal things, was it stealing from the creditors? And how much room would Aunt Sarah have? Would she be offended if I brought too much?

Now she seemed to blame me for leaving too much behind.

There was a knock at the door. Althea Brand stood just outside. She had ridden up behind us in John Gale's wagon, and she looked dusty and small.

"Come in," I said as she hesitated in the doorway.

"I just wanted to tell you good-bye, Harriet, and—"

"I want to give you a present," I said, interrupting. It had just come to me how good she'd been. She didn't have to take care of me. She wasn't even a relative. But she was Mother's friend, and she'd done what a friend should, just out of love.

"Here!" I said, snatching the green teapot from its shelf. Father gave the pot to Mother. It came from Boston, and before that, from China.

"Mother would want you to have it," I said.

Althea's eyes filled with tears. She sat down suddenly at the table. "Thank you, Harriet. I'll think of you both—" Her voice choked off.

Aunt Sarah let out an audible breath. "What about these tomato plants?"

"I don't know." I would have given them to Althea, but hers were already started.

"Bring them along," Aunt Sarah said. Uncle Clayton came to the door. "Clayton, those tomatoes!"

He clumped across the kitchen. Aunt Sarah went out.

I've forgotten something! I thought. Without knowing

why, I hurried through the sitting room and opened the door. Mother's bed was bare now, too, and the thick hush was gone from the room. It looked empty and shabby.

I didn't even think, just pulled open the top bureau drawer. There atop the stockings was the shiny leather wallet. "Your father's pocketbook," it was always called, and she never would make or buy anything prettier to carry her money in.

I pushed it into my pocket and walked out.

When I went to the barn for the colt's halter, I saw other things I'd been forgetting: brushes, bridles, liniment, and buckets. Uncle Clayton would have all those things, but these were mine, and there was my saddle on its peg. I began packing the gear into the buckets. It was dark and cool inside the barn. Behind me I could sense the warm sun and Aunt Sarah's hurry.

My calm surprised me. I had just come from my mother's funeral. How could I be doing this? John Gale came to the barn door. I gave him the two buckets, took the saddle and halter, and followed him to the wagon, wondering: What happened to Belle's harness? Did anyone take it off her, or was it not worth saving?

The colt stood at the gate, leaning so hard that the top bar made a cracking sound. He barely noticed me putting on the halter; all his attention was for the other horses. When I let down the bars, he jumped over them, almost pulling me off my feet.

"Whoa!" I couldn't stop him. He circled me, his head turned toward the horses. I meant no more to him than a post. "Whoa!" I cried. My voice came high and shrill. He would know—everyone would know—that I was afraid.

"Hang on!" Uncle Clayton said, somewhere on the edge of things. "By jing, he's a wild un! Keep hold—"

"Easy, boy." Big brown hands appeared above mine on the rope. "Easy." John Gale.

I didn't want to let go, but there was no room for me, and no need. Gale gave a couple of rough jerks on the halter, and the colt seemed to notice that someone had hold of him. His bright eyes remained fixed on the other horses, but he pranced beside John Gale without pulling. There was nothing left for me to do but follow them up the hill. My legs felt loose, and my throat hurt. The colt had always been so easy to handle. His wildness now felt like betrayal.

John Gale tied the colt's rope to a stout ring at the back of the wagon. The colt pushed against the tailgate, straining toward the broad rumps of the team. "Someone ought to ride with me," Gale said, looking doubtfully at me. "In case he gives me trouble."

"Clayton," Aunt Sarah said.

Then I must ride with Aunt Sarah. I walked quickly to the buggy, determined not to stop, not to look at the house.

I saw it anyway, gray and fragile as a wasp's nest, the worn clapboards gleaming in the sunshine. The geraniums looked out the kitchen window, and Althea Brand stood in the doorway, small and shabby like the house, clutching the teapot to her stomach. I waved and felt tears starting.

No. I pressed my hand hard against my mouth and climbed into the buggy beside Aunt Sarah. She turned the horse, and we started up the long hill.

five

Mother and I spent our lives in West Barrett and downhill. Only in August did we go up, to comb abandoned pastures for blackberries.

But we had come from uphill. The house I traveled to now was the one in which my father had been born and raised. Close to it was the little place he'd lived in with Mother and where I was born.

We climbed slowly through the pastureland, past farms and cornfields. The road was rutted from the recent mud season, dry enough for easy travel but not yet dusty. A couple of miles up, birches were beginning to take over some of the pastures. Their white trunks and lacy leaves made the grass look rich and green. We passed a cellar hole. The house had collapsed into it, and columbines grew over the silver clapboards.

"Whoa!" Aunt Sarah said suddenly. She pointed.

"What?"

"*There!*" she said, pointing harder. Down across a pasture a red-brown animal wandered through a birch grove.

"A—a *deer*?" I'd never seen a deer.

"We see them once in a while now," Aunt Sarah

said. "She'll be in your uncle's bean field next!" She drove on.

We came out into the open now, and an empty green hillside stretched above us. I could see stone walls, and after a minute I saw a house.

It was yellow-gray, the color of goldenrod gone to seed, a two-story Cape with a big front door and a long ell. Beside it stood a gray barn fronted by a muddy yard. Cattle grazed on the slope below.

We crawled up the edge of this pasture until we came to a lane, and then along the lane to the farmyard. The horse stopped of his own accord at the barn door, and Aunt Sarah got out. Numbly I followed.

John Gale's wagon stopped behind us. The colt bobbed his head up, bumping against the tether. His eyes blazed. He'd never been outside West Barrett. The shelf of pasture and the riverbank had been his world.

Hugging myself, I walked back to him. He paid no attention, just twisted and turned and blew hot breath out of huge, reddened nostrils. Could I approach him? I seemed to see myself from above, and I didn't think so: thin and small and thirteen years old. A girl. An orphan.

As I hesitated, Uncle Clayton let himself down from the wagon seat and came back. He untied the rope, and the colt wheeled around him, coat flashing in the sun. His hooves cut the packed dirt.

Out in the pasture a horse whinnied. The colt flung his head high. He listened desperately for a moment. Then his eye seemed to soften with gladness, and he sent a ringing neigh out across the hillside.

He thinks it's Belle. My tears released again.

Through a blur I saw Uncle Clayton stumble toward the barway in the colt's wake. He slipped back the rails, let the colt through, and unclipped the rope.

The colt thundered down the hill in a violent blur of speed, neighing crazily. A blaze-faced work team trotted to meet him. He nearly crashed into them, and all three stood nose to nose. The colt sniffed first one, then the other. Then he raised his head and looked uphill.

Aunt Sarah had led the white horse to the barway. No horse could look less like Belle, but the colt screamed and raced back. The white horse ignored him, buckled his knees, and rolled.

The colt pranced around the rolling animal. His tail stuck straight up and streamed over his back. He still hoped . . . somehow he still hoped that one of these horses was Belle. I hugged myself.

"Hey!" said John Gale, on the wagon seat behind me. "Look!" He pointed toward the top of the barn. I followed his hand and saw a weather vane, a trotting Morgan, with high head and flowing tail.

"Oh." I looked downhill at the colt again. The weather vane Morgan was mature, deep-bodied, and my colt was young and weedy, but the look was there.

"Yes." John Gale drew a breath and let it out slowly, gazing around him. "Decent land," he said, "for hill land."

To me it looked shabby, as if there were more work here than two people could do.

I got two of my carpetbags out of the buggy and, weighed down with them, followed Aunt Sarah into the kitchen. It smelled of vinegar. The table was covered with oilcloth, and a yellow flystrip hung down, several dead flies sticking to it. But every surface shone. It was clean, with that peculiar smell cider vinegar makes when you wash up with it.

Aunt Sarah crossed the kitchen and opened a door onto a set of stairs. They were closed in and dark, turning a corner three-fourths of the way up and continuing a little more steeply. Any light from above was blotted out by Aunt Sarah's bulk.

My breath came shallowly, not seeming to get past my throat. I pressed my palm to the center of my chest and followed.

We came out into the light, in a narrow, steep-shouldered room not much different in shape from my room at home. Everything seemed gray: plaster walls, iron bedstead made up with a gray wool blanket, limp gauze curtains at the window. The vinegar smell was strong here.

It's like a hired man's room! I thought.

Aunt Sarah put the bags on the bed and turned to me, with the nearest thing to a smile I'd seen on her face. "This was your father's room," she said. "I thought you'd like to have it."

A hot feeling flooded my chest. I couldn't speak. I crossed the bare floor, listening to the sound of my bootheels, and looked out the window. The barnyard was below. A red hen scratched in the dung.

"Thank you," I made myself say. My voice came hard and raspy.

There was no answer. I turned. Aunt Sarah just stood there, not gimleting me with her eyes, as I'd expected, but looking at the room.

All at once she noticed me staring. "It'll look prettier

when you've put your things around," she said, and turned toward the stairs.

My things. I sat on the bed beside my carpetbags. I hadn't brought my rug. I hadn't brought the little jug we filled with wildflowers all summer. I'd left all the pictures on the walls. What did I have in these bags except clothing? I didn't want to open them. My hands felt too weak to work the buckles.

Downstairs I heard shuffling feet. Uncle Clayton and John Gale must be walking the sewing machine in. A thump. Now their steps sounded lighter, heading out the door. I went down to say good-bye.

John Gale stood at his horses' heads, looking uncomfortable again. I tried to think what Mother would do, and then I walked over and held out my hand.

"Thank you."

He stood holding my hand, looking down at it. His hand was hard and rough, with dirt ground in so deeply that scrubbing couldn't take it out, though otherwise he seemed like a clean man.

He heaved a sigh, as if trying to push a weight off his chest. "Miss Gibson . . . Miss—" He shook his head. "I'm as sorry as I can be." He gave my hand a squeeze and then climbed up into his wagon and turned it.

I stood watching it rattle down the lane. He turned down the rutted road to the valley and his own concerns. He would pass our house in West Barrett and the flattened place in the grass, go down the broad street by the Academy.

Aunt Sarah said, "Clayton, what time is it? I don't know whether I'm afoot or horseback!"

Uncle Clayton began fishing his watch out of his

pocket. It seemed to hang on a very long chain. "Ha' past four," he said when he'd flipped the watch open and blinked at its face for a few moments.

"Then you've got time to fix that pigpen gate before you milk."

"Guess so."

"Go change your clothes, and I'll fix something to eat." She seemed to push us before her into the kitchen. Uncle Clayton disappeared into another part of the house. Aunt Sarah tied on an apron and began slicing bread.

"Shall I help you?"

She raised her head as if surprised and looked at me for a moment with the knife poised over the loaf. "No. Thank you. Take a look around, why don't you? See where you're at."

My fingers twisted together, making all the little, inflamed stab wounds sting and throb. Look around. Was that what you were supposed to do on the afternoon of your mother's funeral?

I looked into the next room. It should have been the dining room, but Aunt Sarah had arranged it as a sitting room, with rocking chairs, a knitting basket, and a sewing machine in one corner. Not Mother's machine. I didn't see that anywhere.

A door at the back of the room opened, and out came Uncle Clayton, in overalls. Without the jacket I could see how his shoulders sloped. They didn't make a broad shelf, like Dr. Vesper's or John Gale's. They just fell away like the shoulders of a milk bottle.

He seemed embarrassed to see me and gestured vaguely at the room. "Yup, this here's the sittin' room . . . have to get an extra chair in here, I guess."

He opened another door. I glimpsed a hall, bright with sunlight. The knees of a stairway intruded on the left. Beyond was another large room, piled nearly to the ceiling with furniture. I saw beds, tables, couches, a forest of chairs, and, just inside the door, Mother's sewing machine.

The hallway was cold. Cold air flowed down the stairwell and brought with it a smell of vinegar and soda. From deep in the thicket of furniture came a scrabbling sound, like tiny claws on bare wood.

Uncle Clayton waded into the furniture. Dust streamed up through the sunbeams as he put aside a set of hatboxes and three kitchen chairs. He came to grips with a straight-backed rocker and tried to lift it out. It caught on something, and his shoulders worked as he heaved at it.

"Clayton! You'll break it! Wait a minute!"

Uncle Clayton stepped back obediently. Aunt Sarah shoved something, tilted something else, and lifted the rocker straight up in one firm hand.

"There! If you'd use your head for something besides a hatrack— Now take it from me, will you?"

Uncle Clayton started forward guiltily and took the chair. As I stepped out of his way, I gained a new angle on the room. There was a fireplace. Gray and sepia faces frowned down from the walls: two men in uniforms from the time of the Civil War, a severe, heavy-jawed woman with practically no hair.

Aunt Sarah pushed Mother's sewing machine an inch or two deeper into the room and closed the door. "Come and eat," she said, as if none of this required explanation.

Was it like this when my father was a little boy? I'll have to ask Mother, I thought, and then remembered.

six

The mirror in my father's room was murky and speckled. The girl who passed in front of it was the girl I'd glimpsed approaching the colt, the orphan. Her hair was done in two tight braids. Her face was a pale blur, with large dark eyes and a small mouth.

What kept catching my eye, and surprising me, was her dress, a leafy print with bright red berries. Didn't the orphan have anything more suitable?

Even away from the mirror I watched that girl. She sat silently at the table. She didn't ask for anything, took only what was passed. She couldn't seem to mark time properly. Did several days pass, or just one long day? In bed she lay with her eyes wide open. The lump in her chest was too hard for crying.

One morning the girl's aunt asked her to collect eggs. She tried to listen as she was told where to look. But out in the barnyard she remembered nothing. She stood among the crooning, scratching hens with her basket hanging at her side.

A hen strolled from behind the manure pile, clucking loudly. The orphan retraced this path, and in a sheltered spot by the side of the barn she found an egg. She picked it up and turned around.

A rooster's head, with gray, closed lids and gaping beak, lay on the manure pile.

I dropped the egg.

"Harriet! For crying out loud, give me the basket! Now follow me. I'll *show* you where to look."

Nooks and crannies all over the farm—that was where to look, because the hens roamed everywhere. Aunt Sarah even climbed into the haymow. She stooped and peered under the buggy. "Crawl in there for me, Harriet, will you?"

I crawled in. The egg felt warm. I would have liked to cradle it for a while, cup my hands gently around it. But this egg must go in Aunt Sarah's basket.

"That's all, unless they have a nest I don't know about."

I forced myself to speak. "Thank you for showing me."

She was counting her eggs, head bent and chin compressed into two large pillows. "That's all right." Her voice seemed forced, too. "Time to start dinner," she said after a minute. "We always have a big dinner on Sunday."

Sunday dinner. It was Sunday. I watched Aunt Sarah go away, puzzled at her stiffness. It was as if she were shy and on her best behavior. But this was her home. Why would she put on company manners?

Nearby, hens mused over things they found in the dirt. Roosters crowed. The horses and cattle grazed far down the field, the colt glowing among them like a new copper penny. He didn't answer my whistle.

I wandered to the sunny front of the barn and sat on the chopping block. A gray rooster approached. I've met some mean roosters. I pulled my feet back, wondering what this one intended.

He tilted his head and looked at me. Then he noticed a tiny feather on the packed dirt. He viewed it through one eye and then the other and began to chortle. *Ohhh, my, looklooklooklooklooklook!* He pecked the feather, ejected it with a headshake that set his dewlaps wobbling, then pecked it again.

I felt a deep breath lift my ribs. The sun warmed my face and shimmered on the rooster's feathers. *Ohhh, looklooklook!*

I raised my head, and saw for the first time that I was looking down on mountains. Or ridges, anyway, row on row of them, like ocean waves. They receded into the distance, each one a paler, more transparent blue. In the valleys morning mist still lingered, rising like whipped cream out of a bowl.

A high place. I thought of my skyscraper bedroom, where I had looked down on the backs of swallows. I looked quickly away, at the mustard-colored house and drab barn and the hill rising behind it, fringed with birches.

It was silent here. No mill saw, no river, no road for anyone to pass on. Somewhere along this ridge were the little house we lived in when I was too small to remember and the school where Mother was teaching when she and Father met. But were there any people, anywhere?

"Oh, Mother," I whispered. "Why did you send me here?" I felt proud of how I'd done at home. I'd grieved, without entirely forgetting the feelings of other people. I'd been wholehearted, brave, responsible.

Here I felt myself shrinking down. The orphan with her two braids, hunched on a stump. She really should be wearing brown.

Ohhh, look, the rooster remarked. As I watched him peck the feather, I saw in my mind the severed head on the manure pile, with its fringe of bruised and blackened feathers. . . .

The chicken roasting in the kitchen.

The chopping block!

I rose, to a *chuck-chuck-chuck* from the gray rooster, and felt the back of my dress. It was damp, and my hand came away stained with blood.

"Oh, no!" I almost sat down again and let everything close over me like dark wool. But as I bent, I saw the red berries on my skirt. "Don't they just make you *happy,* Harry?" Mother said when we chose the calico. "Let's have dresses just alike, so we can look at each other and be cheerful!"

Mother *chose* to be happy. I never understood that before.

"Ow!" The rooster was pecking my leg. I drew back to kick him, then realized what he was doing. He was pecking the berries.

"They're cloth," I said, drawing back. "They're not real."

He tilted his head to look at me through the other eye, as if much struck. Then he turned back to the ground and the tiny golden feather.

"Watch out for that, too," I said. "That's probably a bad omen."

In the kitchen the roast chicken smell was heavy. Aunt Sarah stood in her pantry, stirring. In the sitting room Uncle Clayton sat collapsed to one side, snoring gently.

At home I would know what to do. Here I wasn't sure what was allowed. "Aunt Sarah?"

She turned her head.

"I've got . . . blood." I held out the wet part of my skirt. "Should I—"

"Good heavens!" She dusted her hands on her apron and came out. "Is it your first time? Are you prepared?"

"Am I *prepared*?" I stared at her large red face. "Prepared for—*oh!*" She thought I'd been taken unawares by my monthly period. "I sat on the chopping block," I said.

Her face flushed even redder. "Well, goodness gracious, go to the sink and pump cold water on it! Surely you know how to do that!"

"That's exactly what I was *going* to do!" I said. "I wanted to make sure you didn't mind!"

Her eyes brightened with anger. I felt how large she was, and my back stiffened. After a moment she folded her lips, swelling with a long, slow breath. "This is your home. You do what you need to."

An especially loud snore sounded in the other room, and a startled "What?"

"Nothing," Aunt Sarah said, turning back to the pantry. "Go on with your reading."

I rinsed the blood out of my skirt and stood with my back to the cookstove to dry it, looking around the clean, ugly kitchen. I felt shaken by the brush with Aunt Sarah. Was this going to be my life, quarreling with her over every little thing?

No, my life would be different. I would have a career,

like Luke's sister, Vicky, who worked for a publisher. That was why schooling was so important.

Instantly Barrett Academy formed in my mind, complete with chalk dust; Miss Spencer's voice fading to a background drone when the algebra got too hard; the smell of horehound cough drops; Luke; and the little society the Academy made, with its teachers, the students from hill farms who boarded at Webb House, town kids who walked or drove in each morning. . . .

I felt the blood drain out of my head. I stared out the window at the transparent waves of ridges.

"Aunt Sarah!"

"Now what?"

"Aunt Sarah, how—how will I get to school?"

There was a pause. She came to the pantry doorway. "School? You've finished school, haven't you? I understood you were through eighth grade."

"I'm at the Academy now, but how am I going to get there? Mother used to drive me—"

Two red spots burned on Aunt Sarah's cheeks. "You don't imagine *we're* going to drive you, do you? It's seven miles each way!"

"But what am I going to *do*?"

"*Do*? There's nothing *to* do! You'll stay right here and take up the life the Lord's given you!"

"I'll drive myself! I can drive—"

"Your uncle needs all three horses right here!"

I became aware of Uncle Clayton in the sitting-room doorway. He was shaking his head at me in some kind of warning. I looked back at Aunt Sarah. "Then I'll board there, I can stay at Webb—"

"And how would you pay for that? If you've got any

money coming to you, girl, I've yet to hear of it! All I've heard about is debts!"

"But—" I didn't have words to go on with. Our lives had revolved around my schooling. Mother always made it the most important thing, and to Aunt Sarah it was nothing.

"I'm sorry," she said after a minute. Her voice had that forced-out sound again, or maybe it was forced *in*, holding things back. "It seems hard, but you have to face facts."

On the flypaper over the table a fly whined and whirred its wings in vain. I stared into Aunt Sarah's marble eyes. "Well, this is a fact," I said. My voice shook. "Mother wanted me to go to school."

Smack! Aunt Sarah hit the table with her open palm. "If your mother is an example of what education does for a woman, I'd like to see the schools close right down!"

My mouth hung open. The chicken sizzled in the oven. After a moment I asked, "What?" My voice came in a whisper. "What?"

Aunt Sarah pressed her lips together, as if trying to prevent more angry words from escaping. "Never mind."

"No! You tell me what you meant by that!"

Aunt Sarah's eyes widened, "I'll tell you what I mean! Your mother was an immoral woman! She got herself in trouble like any common trash, and she ruined my brother's life!"

"Sairy—" Uncle Clayton said, but my voice trampled his.

"What are you talking about?" My voice came full throated now, from the deepest part of my lungs. In one detached corner of my mind I was amazed. I'd never spoken this way to a grown-up, hardly ever to anyone. Aunt Sarah's arm twitched back as if she wanted to slap me. I stepped closer. *"What?"*

"If you're so smart," she said between her teeth, "then when is your birthday? When were your parents married? It doesn't take algebra to figure out that sum!"

I could only stare. After a minute I said, "I don't know when they were married."

"It was too darned late, I can tell you that!"

I understood what she was saying. She was saying that Mother was pregnant when she and Father married. I looked her square in the eye. "My mother was a wonderful person," I said. "The only mistake she ever made was sending me to you!"

At that she did slap me, right across the face. I hardly felt it. It was only a sound.

"Go to your room!"

I turned without speaking and rapidly climbed the stairs. I went straight to the mirror and looked at myself.

The orphan was gone. This girl had brilliant, glittering eyes and one cheek redder than the other. She looked so full of power that she might burst into flames at any moment.

I looked at her. I touched the reddened cheek.

"I will not stay here."

seven

I found a pencil and a tablet of the ugly paper we used for algebra.

> Dr. Vesper [I wrote],
> I will not stay here and listen to my mother being insulted. May I come and live with you? I will work hard and do everything I can not to be a burden.
> Please come see me as soon as you can.
> > Your grateful friend,
> > Harriet Gibson

I folded it and addressed the outside. Now I began to hear the sounds downstairs: the ongoing angry rumble of Aunt Sarah's voice, an occasional protest from Uncle Clayton.

I went down. Aunt Sarah rounded at the sound of my step. "I thought I told you to go upstairs!"

I looked past her. "Uncle Clayton, I need this letter to go to Dr. Vesper. When do you go down for your mail?"

He looked away from me, only to recoil from Aunt Sarah's expression. "Wednesdays!"

Three more days. I looked out the window. Clouds lay in combed rows across the eastern sky, mirroring the rows of ridgetops. Below the pasture I saw the slender brown line of the road.

"Never mind." I walked out the front door.

The air felt cool. A rim of blue sky showed in the east, but from the west bigger, darker clouds were pushing in. I headed straight across the yard. Hens scattered. Only the gray rooster hesitated, eyeing the red berries on my dress. *Ohh, look.*

I plunged past him, along the rutted lane. Wind clapped the maple leaves. Down in the pasture the colt flung his head high and watched me. He hadn't given up hope that any moving creature might be his mother.

"I'll be back for you," I said to him. Everything was clear in my mind. I would walk down to West Barrett and stay the night with Althea Brand. In the morning I'd see Dr. Vesper and the lawyer, and I would figure out what to do next. I'd work as a hired girl rather than come back here. I'd live in a *barn*—

Something rumbled. I turned. Behind the row of maples loomed an enormous crinkled cloud. The rumble came again.

One thing I'd been well taught was to seek shelter at the first sign of a thunderstorm. I hesitated. I wasn't out of sight of the house yet.

But it was no part of my plan to be hit by lightning. I turned and walked toward the barn, ignoring the face at the kitchen window. The first fat raindrops were spearing into the dirt as I reached the haymow door.

Hens ran into the barn after me as the rain began to sheet down. I sat among them. The gray rooster strolled close. I picked up a handful of the chaff that lay all around me, dusty and golden, and held it out to him.

He drew back and pecked shrewdly at the chaff on the floor. What's so special about yours? he seemed to be asking. He scratched a long trough with one foot and inspected the results.

I looked past him, out the big door. The rain beat down. The stinging nettles bent and dripped. *Crack!* of lightning, thunder like a freight train on an iron bridge.

Against this background I saw myself arriving hot and sweaty at Althea Brand's. I saw myself on Dr. Vesper's doorstep, demanding shelter. I saw the looks on their faces.

No, not that way. Send the letter and wait.

A shower of chaff buried my foot. The rooster had drawn his line there, and now he pecked importantly, pretending to pay no attention to me. I tipped my hand to show him my chaff, and he drew back in alarm. I thought of Aunt Sarah's hand twitching back to hit me and how I had stepped forward to meet the blow. That side of my face hurt. I had never been slapped before.

I'd never been that angry.

"I don't believe it," I said. "It isn't true!" Everything Mother did was open, joyful, courageous. I couldn't imagine her getting married because she had to.

So why was Aunt Sarah lying? Why exactly did she hate Mother?

Mother was young, I thought, and full of charm, and educated. She was different, and people are like chickens.

Tears prickled my eyes. I could hear her saying, "People are like chickens, Harry. They'll always peck the one that's different."

My throat felt full and tight. Through my tears I watched the hens, so pretty with their wide, plump bodies and their tiny, tiny heads. We were both different, especially here where Aunt Sarah ruled. While Mother was alive, she protected me, but now I was getting pecked, too.

So why did she send me here?

Across the yard rain streamed out the eaves' spout and splashed into a barrel at the corner of the house. Smoke flattened black under the rain, puffed down, and tried to rise again. My father lived right here, as a boy. But I didn't remember my father. Being where he grew up couldn't make me happy.

Was it just that Mother thought Aunt Sarah *should* take care of me? That didn't sound like Mother. If there was one thing I knew, it was that Mother loved me more than anything in the world. She must have thought this was best for me.

"But *why*?" I tipped my head back and spoke up toward the blackness. "Mother, why?"

Suddenly I felt something touch my hand. I looked down. The rooster was just drawing back as if he thought himself very clever, with a large piece of chaff in his beak. He crooned, *Ohh, mymymymy. Ohh, my—*

"You're funny," I told him. My voice was achy and rasping, but I could feel myself almost smile. I looked down at the letter in my hand, and I heard Dr. Vesper saying, "It's what Ellen wanted. They owe it to her to try."

I hadn't really tried at all yet. I'd just barely woken up, had just started to see where I was and who was here with me. In a way it felt worse than the gray zone where the orphan lived. It *hurt*. My throat ached with sorrow. But I was awake now, and I would try. One thing I knew, though: Mother wouldn't want me to stay here if it meant giving up my education.

Exams must be soon, I thought. Next week? Could I go down and take them? Could I afford the Academy? And how could I get there? Could I possibly train the colt by next fall and ride him down?

Dr. Vesper could answer some of those questions. Only I could answer the last one. I always meant to train him, I thought. I'll just have to get started.

eight

The rain stopped. The sun came out through the last long, fat drops and shone on the puddles as I crossed the yard.

They were eating. A place was set for me. I sat down, and Aunt Sarah served me without speaking. To my surprise I was hungry, and I didn't mind eating that rooster, though I'd seen his head on the manure pile and though he was cooked dry. Mother was a better cook than Aunt Sarah—not that we often aspired to a chicken. Popcorn and milk was our Sunday dinner.

I looked up and caught Uncle Clayton glancing from Aunt Sarah to me. He started when he met my eyes, and reached for another biscuit.

When the meal was finished, I helped Aunt Sarah clear away and wash dishes. It was while I was drying the platter that she finally spoke. "We'll have to learn to get along better." She was scrubbing the bottom of the roasting pan, with her big chin pillowed and her mouth tight.

We? I thought. Who started it? But it was the nearest she could come to an apology. I could understand that. I hate apologies, too. "Yes," I said finally, "we will."

That began a week of dancing: two steps forward, two back. No, I don't want your help with washing; then a brooding, emotion-filled silence the next day, until I understood that I *was* supposed to help iron.

Spend more time outdoors.

Where were you?

Where I was all Tuesday afternoon was trying to catch the colt. He'd always been friendly before, sometimes too friendly, dogging our heels when we caught Belle or repaired the fence. But the freedom of the big pasture had gone to his head, or else a week or so of neglect had caused him to forget me. He let me get close, but not close enough, until I lost my temper and threw the rope at him. Then he kicked up his heels and galloped away.

Wednesday Uncle Clayton went for the mail. He took two letters from me, one to the Academy, asking about examinations, and one to Dr. Vesper, asking him to explain the exact state of my finances. Aunt Sarah looked sharply when I handed the letters over but asked no questions.

I helped her bake. Heat rolled off the big stove, but she kept me well away from it. Not with any expression of tenderness; she just set me to work at the far table and watched sharply as I rolled out piecrust.

"You have a nice light hand," she commented. I heard the note of surprise and understood it for yet another insult to Mother. I pressed my lips together and didn't answer.

After a minute she said, "It's a nice day out. Go get some fresh air."

The kitchen was hot and dark, and sun shone outside

the windows, but Aunt Sarah's voice made me want to stay right there at the table just to spite her.

Instead I went down into the pasture with a rope and a measure of oats. The colt flung up his head and watched me, but the work team only tipped their ears and kept on grazing. I went halfway down the hill and rattled the oats.

All across the field heads lifted. Ears pointed at me: cow ears and horse ears. I hadn't expected them all to notice, but the colt was looking, too. I shook the oats again, softly.

A cow stepped toward me. Like the slow start of an avalanche, others stepped, glanced at one another, sped up, until they all were trotting, shaking their big fringed ears, bucking, cantering. Now the horses came at a gallop.

I fled toward the gate, but two speckled heifers blocked the way. Hooves thundered behind me. I froze and ducked my head. When nothing hit me, I turned, and the team reached their big noses to the oats. The colt veered past them and started a swirl of cows milling around me.

"Bess! Chick! Go on!" I heard a popping sound. Cows galumphed away to either side, and the horses backed up, flattening their ears. Then Aunt Sarah was beside me, large and hot, with a buggy whip in her hand.

"*Thank* you!" I said.

But Aunt Sarah looked into the measure. "Why on earth are you feeding good oats to these animals? There's plenty of grass!"

"I was trying to catch the colt—" I stopped myself. I hated the weak, excusing sound of my voice, as if I didn't have a perfect right to do what I was doing.

"Oh, so now he can't be caught?"

"I'll catch him," I said as we made for the gate.

"Well, don't waste good oats. They're too hard come by." Aunt Sarah drew the bars back. How had she gotten in? I wondered. Did she slip between the rails or climb?

"Try apples next time," she suggested after a moment. "Might be a little more private!"

I looked at her quickly. That was almost a joke. "Thank you. Where are the apples?"

"In a bin down cellar. I'll show you." She paused. "What do you call that animal?"

We are having a conversation! I thought. "We—he doesn't really have a name." We could never decide on one. We were always reading a new novel with a new hero and trying that name. He was Laurie once, from *Little Women.* "I call him Kid," I said, just to keep things going.

"I see."

The gray rooster jerked a shrewd glance upward as we approached. I offered him oats on the palm of my hand.

Ohhh, looklooklook. He came close, and I saw how beautiful his eye was, the green center surrounded by hot orange. He snatched an oat. I felt his wattle touch my fingers, and high above, Aunt Sarah cleared her throat.

"I hope you know better than to make a pet of a farm animal."

I ignored her, shaking the oats farther down my fingers. Above my head I heard a massive indrawn breath, and then she swept on ahead of me, toward the house.

She gave me some wizened russet apples, and I spent the afternoon by the brook. In the lacy shade of the birches

I waited until the horses came to rest and drink. Then I ate an apple loudly.

The colt couldn't bear it long. He came and begged with an eloquent nose. I made him wait for the core, and I didn't even try to touch his halter. Instead I walked away, eating another apple. He followed and nudged, and at last I gave it to him.

I put my hand on the halter then, and scratched his ears, but made no attempt to hold him. The next day, when I went down with apples in my pockets, he came right to me.

I didn't know what to do with him once I had him. Once I'd had a plan. I had a book by Dennis Magner, the great horse tamer, and I was going to follow his directions, and the colt was going to be perfectly trained. People were going to marvel at how well a young girl had done. Now I led the colt around in a few circles, let him loose, and went for a walk.

The lane meandered past the barn to the crest of the hill. An old road ran along there, so rarely used that it was mostly grassed over. I followed it, passing another abandoned cellar hole, and after a while came upon a small brick building with a hole in the roof and a padlock on the door.

I peeked in one cobwebbed window. Rows of empty desks faced a blackboard. This must be the school Mother taught in. Here she first met my father.

I sat on the front step. They must have sat here together, after the children had gone home. There were only three children then, on all this broad hillside. It was an easy school to teach, Mother used to say, and in the afternoons Father came.

I looked off at the blue hills. She would like to know I was here. Maybe she did know. I could almost feel her shoulder nudging mine, and I stayed as long as the feeling lasted. The hills were dusky purple when I walked back along the ridge.

"Where in heaven's name have you been?" Aunt Sarah shattered my peace the minute I walked in. I could smell supper, but nothing was on the table.

"I went for a walk."

"And how was I to know that?"

Of course there was no answer. I should have told her. I faced down her angry eyes.

I would have told Mother because Mother loved me. Mother would worry. Aunt Sarah only wanted to be the boss.

nine

The nights were worse than the days. Aunt Sarah and Uncle Clayton went to bed at nine, and I was meant to go, too. When they'd closed their bedroom door, the house was silent. It was too quiet to turn in bed, too quiet to cry. Night after night I lay still and narrow, like a wrinkle in the blanket. I could hear how big that house was. I could sense its rooms crowded with ghostly furniture. Sometimes I was cold, sometimes I broke into a sweat, because it was real. It was true. Mother was dead.

Every time I got in bed I prayed that she'd come back in another dream, and dreams did come, but they were never like that first one. That one was *her*, and the dreams I had now were only me, trying to rearrange things in my mind.

Thank goodness for Aunt Sarah, I sometimes thought. All day long I braced against her. That was eighteen hours out of every twenty-four when I felt strong and wary and a little mean, and that was better than feeling crushed. How would I hold out, I wondered, when I was with someone who loved me? Uneasily I watched the road for my first visitor.

No one came.

Luke was at school, I reminded myself, and Althea Brand had no way to come, and Dr. Vesper was busy. But on Saturday there was no school. Luke would be missing me. All morning, as I collected eggs, and led the colt in the pasture, and helped Aunt Sarah get dinner, and ate dinner, I was really down in Barrett watching Luke. She woke up—and as the day wore on, I woke her later and later in my mind—and negotiated to use Tulip, their phlegmatic horse. Maybe Mrs. Mitchell needed Tulip first. Maybe Vicky had come home, and there were family doings. But surely by lunchtime, or right after lunch, Luke was saddling and riding up the road. With her I turned my face away at the place where the grass was crushed, and with her tears sprang to my eyes as I went by our little gray house. Then up the silent hill, arriving just about two o'clock.

Tulip was a slow horse. Say three o'clock, or half past.

At four o'clock I was waiting hunched on the chopping block, my arms pressed tight against the hot, crawling sensation in my stomach. By five o'clock I knew: out of sight, out of mind. My friends might care while I was there in front of them, but they didn't care enough to come this far. Here I was, and here I'd rot, as far as anyone in Barrett was concerned.

In the barn milk hissed into Uncle Clayton's pails. My rooster pecked near my feet, the only creature in the world that willingly sought my company.

Two by two Uncle Clayton carried the milk pails to the house. When he came to let the cows out, Aunt Sarah came, too. "We need a bird for Sunday dinner," she said, and reached down and grabbed the gray rooster by the legs. He gave a squawk and hung blinking from her hand.

I stood up. "That's *my* rooster!"

Aunt Sarah barely glanced at me. "You can't get attached to farm animals. They aren't pets." She handed the upside-down rooster to Uncle Clayton and started to turn away. I felt the lump in my chest swell and crack.

"You have a dozen roosters! Kill one of the others!"

Aunt Sarah paused, stiffening. "Harriet," she said, "these are my chickens. I'll manage them as I see fit."

Something seemed to burst inside me. I stamped my foot. "You don't want me to have anything! You want me to *die!*"

She turned very slowly. Her face was blotched white and red, and she seemed gigantic, like an oceangoing ship. If I'd had any sense, I would have been frightened, but I stood my ground, thrusting my jaw at her. She said, in a voice so soft I could hardly hear it, "Clayton, kill that bird!"

"No!" I said. "Give him to me!"

Uncle Clayton's jaw sagged. He looked from me to Aunt Sarah. The rooster's wings opened in a faint, dazed way.

"Harriet Gibson!" Aunt Sarah said. "You may not have been raised to respect adults, but you're about to learn!"

"I was raised *fine!*" I screamed the last word, so loud it slapped up a little echo off the side of the barn. "I was raised to respect *good* people! But you don't want me to have *any*thing!"

"You've got that colt out there eating his head off! You've got a room of your own! Some children might be grateful, but your mother—"

"You leave my mother out of this!"

"Oh, yes, leave her out! She took my brother away from this farm; she disgraced herself and spoiled his life—"

"That is *not* true! You're lying!"

"Oh, look in your Bible, child! Read the dates!" She turned away from me contemptuously. "Clayton!"

I pushed past her and snatched the rooster out of his unresisting hand. The bird's legs were warm. I tipped him gently upright and settled him under my arm. "I'll be back for my things when I've found a place to live." My voice shook, but it sounded clear and brave. I turned and started down the lane.

I didn't see anything. I didn't hear. My body shook, and in my mind I yelled at Aunt Sarah. I did the whole fight again, only better. "If my mother had been a *bank robber*, she'd still be a better person than you are!" I screamed inside.

It felt glorious.

I stumbled. *Uhh-ohhhh,* the rooster murmured. I felt him shudder in my arms. His head bobbed with every step I took, jerking side to side as he tried to focus. I looked into his green and orange eye. She would have chopped his head off.

"I will never go back," I said. "This time nothing's going to stop me."

The long, low afternoon sun slanted through the trees. I turned down the main road, skirting the lower edge of the big pasture. I would find a place to live, I would send for Mother's sewing machine, and I'd earn a living for myself. She'd taught me to sew a seam; with thought, with practice, I could learn to design as she had, to make the little adjustments that turned an ordinary dress into something far more flattering.

Or I'd go out as a hired girl.

Oh, yes, I can see that! some part of me said, in a voice like Aunt Sarah's. A runaway orphan, as near illegitimate as makes no difference—

"That's a lie!"

Ohh, murmured the rooster. His chest vibrated on my arm. *Ohh, look!* He cocked his head, listening, and now I, too, heard hoofbeats, coming from downhill.

A buggy emerged from the shade of the birches, pulled by a horse I didn't know. We drew nearer each other. In the shadow of the hooded buggy a face began to take shape: an unbleached shirtfront—no, a long yellow-white beard.

The one-armed man.

The horse reached me and stopped of its own accord, puffing. It had deep hollows over its eyes and looked too fuzzy for this time of year, as if it hadn't shed out properly. It turned its head toward the rooster but didn't seem to have enough strength or curiosity to sniff.

I kept walking. As I passed the front wheel, a voice issued out of the dark buggy. "Well, hello there! You'll be Harry Gibson."

I stopped in my tracks. No one had called me Harry in a long time. I stared into the old man's clear, pale eyes and felt a sudden shock, the kind you feel when you miss the bottom stair. I knew him. Didn't I? But who was he?

"Where you goin' with Sarah's rooster?"

The top of my head prickled. "How do you know whose rooster it is?"

Movement beneath the beard seemed to indicate a smile. "Ain't many roosters on this ridge. Where you takin' him?"

Mother taught me not to talk with strange men. I glanced behind me. I could get over the stone wall quickly, if I needed to.

"Don't remember me, do you? It's Truman Hall, your uncle Clayton's brother."

Truman! I remembered the name. I remembered that Uncle Truman had been good to Mother and Father, and suddenly I remembered him, sitting at our kitchen table once or twice when I was very small.

"You came to the funeral."

He nodded. "I'da done better to come while she was alive, but it ain't easy with a horse this old. Jerry's done well to get me down to the birches today." Beneath and behind the seat, I noticed now, were bundles of dry twigs, tied together with strips of rag. "Kindling," Truman said. "I don't split it as easy as some folks." He shrugged his left shoulder, and the shortened arm moved within the sleeve.

"Where do you live?"

"Live in your house," he said. "House where you were born."

"Really? Where is it?"

He pointed uphill with his chin. I saw only the road and the empty green slope. "I was born there, too," he said. "So was your Uncle Clayton. I sold the place to your dad when they got married, bought it back from your mother when he died. You prob'ly don't remember it."

"No. I only remember West Barrett."

"Headin' back there?" Truman asked. "I see you're takin' along your supper!"

I glanced down at the rooster, lying warm and docile on my arm. "No, he—he's friendly. He likes me. She was going to kill him for Sunday dinner!" To my horror tears overflowed my eyes. "She has a dozen roosters, but just because I like this one—" I stopped myself.

Truman shook his head. "Sarah, Sarah, Sarah," he said, in a warm, musing voice. "Always did make bad worse. Little bit that way yourself, ain't you, Harry?"

"No! I never fight with people! It's *her*!"

A huge grin cracked Truman's face. He cocked his head and looked at me with an expression of pure delight. "Y'know, when I see Sarah pickin' you up at the funeral, I says to myself, Trume, I says, Sarah don't know it, but she's got a bobcat by the tail. Ohh, my!"

Ohh, my, the rooster echoed, shifting. I felt his wings try to flap, and I wrapped my arm closer around him.

"Mr. Hall, I need to be going," I said as politely as I could.

He leaned forward. One elbow rested on his knee. The other arm didn't include an elbow. "Now, youngster, listen. Are you dead set on runnin' away?"

"I'm not running away. I'm just leaving."

"Because if you ain't," he said, "it'd give me a lot of pleasure to have you in the neighborhood. Now, tell you what, c'mon up home with me. Bring your bird, and I'll shelter him for you. Then you and me and him can visit back and forth, and we'll study up how to civilize Sarah."

I hesitated. The sun was nearing the ridgetop, and the

road below was deeply shadowed. It was a long way down to West Barrett, and the bird was shifting in my arms.

But would I really get into a buggy with a strange man? Would I really go back to Aunt Sarah a second time, after running away?

"Course, if you come with me, you've got to walk," Truman said. "Jerry'd catch his never-get-over if he had to haul us both."

He chirruped, and stiffly the old horse put himself in motion. I turned with the turning wheel and watched the buggy leaving. The hillside seemed wide and still and empty.

I took three long steps and caught up.

ten

My arm was cramping. I shifted the rooster. He opened his beak, and a screech came out that sounded like *help, help, help!*

Truman dropped the reins on the dash, set his foot on them, and took off his straw hat. He handed it to me. "Put that over his head. He'll feel better if he can't see too much."

The hat was worn and greasy, but the rooster stilled beneath it. I walked beside the wheel, and Truman leaned forward on his one elbow, gazing at the green hillside. He didn't speak. We neared the farm lane and very slowly passed it. I listened for the sound of other hoofbeats. Would Aunt Sarah really let me run away? Wouldn't she come after me?

"If Jerry was younger," Truman said suddenly, "I'd drive up and tell Sarah not to worry. But when a horse hits thirty, he's only got so many steps left in him."

"I *want* her to worry," I said. "It serves her right!"

He grinned again, as if something about me delighted him beyond measure.

We continued up the road about half a mile farther. A grassy lane branched off to the left. Jerry turned in there and stopped with a sigh, dropping his head to graze. Truman climbed down awkwardly and stood patting the old horse, looking across the blue folds of the hills.

I looked, too. We're so high, I thought. It made me feel calm and at home, as if I were looking out my own bedroom window.

"All right, Jerry." Truman pulled up the old horse's head, and we walked on either side of him. The lane seemed untracked and abandoned, but ahead I saw the sagging wall of a shed.

In a moment the whole house came into view: a low gray Cape, crumbling back into the hillside. The shed was swaybacked, and lichen grew on the roof slates, making them look thick and soft. Lilacs crowded tight to the house, and they were blossoming, though the lilacs at home had already faded. A shiver traveled up my spine. I don't remember this, I thought. I'm sure I don't remember.

Truman led Jerry into the shed, which was open on both sides. I watched with an unsettled feeling in my stomach as he unhitched and unharnessed. The lone hand seemed independently alive, like an animal.

He slung the harness onto the wall pegs and slipped the bridle off Jerry's head. Jerry shuddered his skin and ambled out the other side of the shed, down the green slope. I looked out after him. There was no fence in sight, only hens bobbing in the grass, looking like fat old ladies with their hands clasped behind their backs.

"Won't he run away?"

"Jerry ain't ambitious," Truman said. He looked around blankly, scratching in his beard. Then he fetched down a dusty bushel basket from a rafter peg. "Here, stick your bird under this. I'll put him with the hens after dark."

I put the rooster on the ground, and Truman lowered the basket as I took my hands away. A soft, weary *ohhh* and then silence.

I stepped back. Truman said, "Now, Harry. Thirsty?" I nodded.

"Set down on the step, and I'll fetch you a cup of water." He disappeared through a door in the shed, and I went outside.

The front step was a brown piece of sandstone, weathered and soft looking. I sat, curling my legs under me. A low purple-flowered plant with scalloped leaves grew all around the stone. Bees buzzed and stirred the blossoms.

That's gill-go-by-the-ground, I said to myself.

How did I know that? My gaze dropped to the edge of the stone, where a large chip was missing—

The back of my neck prickled. In my mind's eye I saw a baby's finger, pink and pointed, tracing the chip. *My* finger.

The door opened behind me. Cold, dog-smelling air flowed out. A dog came, too, a cow-dog, who flattened her ears at me in a friendly way. Behind her came Truman, with two tin cups in his hand. I took one, and he lowered himself onto the rock beside me. The dog squeezed in between.

"Well now, this is neighborly!"

I drank half my water in two big gulps. It was cold and sweet. "I remember this rock," I said after a minute. "I remember sitting out here."

"I remember you here," Truman said.

The rock was warm, and warmth spread into me. The place seemed to put its arm around me. I cradled the tin cup and looked over the rim, at the crooked, spindling bean poles, green grass and green trees, hills turning from blue to purple.

The dog sighed and nudged at my hands. I put an arm around her, brushing the rough cloth of Truman's coat with my elbow.

"What's her name?"

"Name? Seems to me I named her Nell. Call her Tippy nowadays." The dog flattened her ears at both names. "What you call that horse of yours?"

"He doesn't have a name yet. I call him Kid." I listened to the quietness of the hillside. It was the same hill Aunt Sarah lived on, but here I felt as if I belonged.

"What happened to your arm?" I asked.

The lines around his eyes deepened. "You asked me that the last time I talked to you."

"I don't remember."

"You wa'n't but four or five." Truman glanced down at where his left elbow should have been. "I took a bullet, and they cut it off."

"In the *war*?"

"Well, it ain't *the* war anymore. The War Between the States."

I'd seen the old veterans march in the Decoration Day parade; not very many of them anymore. I'd never seen Truman there. "Did it—did it hurt *terribly*?" It seemed like a stupid question, but I had to ask.

His eyes twinkled. "I can't remember," he said. "Three days later I couldn't remember. Seemed to hurt the other fellers, though, so I suppose it hurt me, too. God arranges so you forget some things, which I guess is a mercy."

I stared. I couldn't begin to imagine having your arm cut off. The worst thing that had ever happened to me was a skinned knee. No. The worst thing that ever happened to me was Mother.

"When did you stop missing it?"

"Miss it yet," he said. "First thing in the mornin', when I reach for my boots. After that—oh, I'm old now anyway. Wouldn't be able to do much even if I had two hands."

"But—" That wasn't really the answer to my question.

After a moment he seemed to understand. "When a thing like that happens, you don't feel it so sharp at first. You're kind of stunned. Then later, oh, Mother of God, it hurt! And you begin to sense how nothing's going to be the same. In a while, though, by the fall after it happened, I decided I was glad to be alive. And then little by little you get better."

I felt Tippy warm against my side, and Truman warm against the arm I had around her. Something inside me relaxed. Just to be understood, to have someone answer an unspoken question . . .

"I wish I could stay here."

Truman nodded slowly. "Come back," he said after a minute. "I'm just about always here."

"I thought someone would come visit me." I heard the hurt in my voice and would rather have hidden it, but the words tumbled out suddenly. "I wrote to Dr. Vesper, and I wrote to the Academy. There'll be exams soon. I thought Luke might—" A big hot air bubble rose in my throat and stifled me.

"Barrett Academy," Truman mused. "Still teach Latin, do they?"

"Yes."

" '*Amo, amas, amat,*' " he quoted. " 'I love, you love' "—and with a glance at Tippy—" 'she loves.' That's about all I remember—no, wait! '*Gallia est omnis divisa in partes tres—*' "

" '*—quarum unam incolunt Belgae!*' "

"Yup, the good old Belgae. That's somethin', isn't it? After all that time there's still a place called Belgium on the map."

"I have to take my exams," I said. "I have to be ready for next year."

"You figure on goin' then?"

I didn't see the hills anymore. I saw Dr. Vesper at the table, and Aunt Sarah standing up like a Roman column, and that long, steep road. "I don't know how," I said. "It's so far, and . . . I don't know how I'll afford it."

Truman's eyes scanned the landscape, with the look of calm delight that was particularly his. "You got time," he suggested.

"No!" I stood up abruptly, and Tippy stood up, too, waving her tail. "Nobody has time, not to be sure of. Look at Mother!"

He nodded slowly, conceding the point.

"And anyway, time—I've been there weeks already and—oh, *why* did she send me there?" Tears poured down my face. "She *hates* us! Aunt Sarah *hates* us! She says horrible things, and—*why*?" I collapsed on the stone again with my face on my knees.

Tippy whined and pawed me. Then she was pushed away, and Truman's arm wrapped around my shoulders.

He let me cry. When I got quiet, he said, "You want to ask yourself, Harry: where else could she send you? Her folks are gone, and Sarah's all that's left of Walter's folks. She had a right to ask Sarah, and she knew Sarah'd do her duty."

"Aunt Sarah hates us," I said in a thready voice, and sniffled massively.

Truman's arm came away. "Walk out back of the house, Harry, and get a handkerchief off the clothesline."

I obeyed. I was startled to see that it was nearly dusk. The bushes were dense shadows, and the last hen walked hastily into the coop.

I found the clothesline. Hanging on it were a pair of overalls, some long underwear, and three blue bandannas, worn so thin I could see my hand right through them. I unpinned one, mopped my itching face, and blew my nose.

"Harry, come give me a hand with this rooster," Truman called from the back door of the shed. I heard him chuckle. "Give me a hand! Think that's funny?"

"Uh—"

"Your ma and Walter always laughed. Sarah just gets mad." His hand curved over the rim of the bushel. When the basket lifted, I closed my hands around the warm, drowsy rooster. I put him in the coop, and Truman closed the door, held it shut with one knee, and turned the peg.

"There! Now, Harry, I know you want Sarah to suffer, but I got to send you back."

I didn't answer. The peepers began their shrill piping somewhere near. It was night.

"I'd go with you," Truman said, "but I can't ask Jerry to make another trip. Tell you what—you take Tippy and keep her overnight. Then, why, I'll have to come fetch her, won't I? Tell Sarah she'll have company to Sunday dinner."

He got a rope from the dark shed and fastened it to Tippy's collar. "Go along now," he said. "I'll see you tomorrow."

I started down the grassy lane. After a minute I heard a shout behind me. I turned, and Truman called, "S'pose we'll have chicken?"

eleven

Beyond the stone walls the world was dark. Tippy and I got ourselves between the ruts, and the road rolled us downhill. I would have passed the farm lane, but Tippy hesitated there and whined.

"Thank you, Tippy." Suddenly I was so tired I could hardly keep walking.

After a few minutes I heard hoofbeats and buggy wheels behind me. Tippy and I stepped to one side and waited. A pale blur, a heavy, sloppy trot—that was Whitey, Uncle Clayton's buggy horse, passing. Ahead a window glowed yellow. I walked toward it as Whitey stopped, the kitchen door opened, and a tall black column filled the rectangle of light.

"Did you find her?"

"She didn't go there. Nobody saw her."

I trudged past the buggy, past the horse. I wanted to walk straight inside and sit, but Aunt Sarah blocked the way. She wore a peculiar expression. I could barely see it, let alone interpret.

"Why, here she is, Sairy!"

"Yes, Clayton, I can see that." Aunt Sarah turned, and I followed her inside. I smelled potatoes and salt pork gravy, and instantly I was famished. I sat at the table. Aunt Sarah brought the pan from the stove. My eyes wouldn't open normally. I squinted up at her.

"Did you leave my rooster up to Truman's?" she asked. How did she know that? I wondered, and then saw Tippy exploring near the stove for crumbs.

"Yes. He said, expect company for dinner tomorrow."

Silence answered me. I managed to widen my eyes and see her, but I couldn't tell anything of what she might be thinking.

Tippy slept on my legs, and for the first time here I slept all night long. I woke to the sound of the dog's toenails on the stairs, feeling . . . not good, not happy, but expecting something, ready to start the day.

After chores Aunt Sarah started cooking dinner, and I went out to catch the colt. He came for his apple, sighed when I caught him, but allowed himself to be led through the gate. I put the bars back up and turned him toward the barn.

In my mind I already had him tied and was putting on the saddle. In his mind the colt was right here, and a strange little two-legged animal was coming toward him. His eyes bulged. He sank back on quivering haunches.

"Oh, for goodness' sake! It's a *hen*!"

But hens didn't roam free in West Barrett, and the colt had never seen one. His forefeet plunged right, left, and he started to back. I hung on, shouting, "Whoa! Whoa!" Two more hens arrived and scratched vigorously at the fresh black hoofmarks. The colt backed against the bars.

"Come *on*!" I pulled on the rope, but he only pressed

backward. The gate began to creak. He'd break it! "Come on!" I yelled. "Come *on*! Come *on*!"

"Easy," someone said behind me. Uncle Clayton was there, gently shooing the hens away. The colt eased off the gate, and his head came down a little.

"Never seen a hen before?"

"I—I guess not." And he had panicked, the way Belle panicked when John Gale's Model T Ford came down West Barrett hill.

The hens began to return, flowing around Uncle Clayton's legs like brook water. The colt's head came down another inch. "He's a smart feller," Uncle Clayton said. "Once he sees what they are, he'll be all right."

He turned back toward the house, leaving me alone with colt and hens and a quivering feeling that spread from my stomach out through my arms and legs. I knew what that feeling was. I was afraid.

I'd seen the broken buggy and Belle beside it, but I hadn't thought much about the moment when the automobile was coming and Mother decided to make Belle face it. The plunging hooves, Belle's sunlit back, the moment when it was too late, when the buggy was tipping and Belle wouldn't stop.

The colt sighed and dropped his head into my shoulder. His bones pressed against mine. I cupped one hand behind his ear, feeling his heat and the quick, leaping pulse. How many other terrifying sights lay between here and the Academy steps?

Just then I heard a squeak and a rattle, and Truman's old buggy appeared at the bend in the lane. Tippy trotted toward it, waving her tail.

The colt's chin drew into a tight, quivering cone. His

ears swiveled, showing the swing of his reactions. At last he tried to bolt. I stood firm, and he trotted in a circle around me.

Truman stopped the buggy. "Harry!" he called. "Tell him, 'Trot!' "

"Trot!" I gasped, expecting somehow that this would stop the colt.

Nothing changed, but Truman said, "Now tell him, 'Good boy!' "

"Why?"

"He done what you told him, didn't he?"

"Good *boy*!" I said, and started laughing. "Trot, darn you! Trot! Good boy!"

Another circle and the colt stopped, staring at Jerry. At a nod from Truman I said, "Whoa! Good boy!," feeling like a fool. The colt continued to stare at Jerry while I maneuvered him through the gate. Released, he came to press against the rails and gaze as I turned back to Truman.

"Is that how *you* train horses? Tell them to do what they're already doing?"

"I don't train horses, but that's part of it. If you can't make 'em do what you want, make 'em think you want what they're doin'."

"I trained him to lead," I said, "and to pick up his feet. But I've never trained a horse to ride."

"No? And you more'n a dozen years old! Get up, Jerry." We headed slowly toward the barn, the colt following along the fence line as long as he could. "How old is that critter?"

"Two."

"That's young. He'll get over a lot of foolishness on

his own if you give him a year." Truman climbed down at the barn door and tousled Tippy's ears.

"I don't have a year. I need to ride him by the end of summer."

Truman looked up. In the shadow of the barn his eyes were green and glassy, like the net floats Luke brought from the seashore. "Doesn't pay to hurry a horse."

I set my lips firmly and didn't answer.

When we'd unhitched Jerry and put him in a stall, we went to the house together. Truman stopped just inside the kitchen door, closed his eyes, and inhaled deeply. "Salt pork gravy! By jing, that smells good!"

Uncle Clayton stood in the sitting-room doorway. He made a small, startled jerk and looked quickly at Aunt Sarah. She was stirring something on the stove, surrounded by billows of steam. I couldn't see that she even glanced up.

Truman sat down at the table and began playing with a fork. Once again I noticed that there was only one hand; it was a moment when a man would naturally have used two. "I never saw a rooster as tame as that," he remarked, raising his voice slightly. "Just a little leery when I opened the door this mornin', but I had him takin' grain out of my hand in ten minutes. Lot of roosters'd just as soon scratch your eyes out—"

Aunt Sarah put a plate of biscuits on the table with a good deal of emphasis. She looked at him for a moment, pressing her lips together. "Truman, if you're looking for an apology, just ask for one!"

Uncle Clayton and I glanced at each other uncomfortably.

"You don't owe *me* an apology," Truman said. "And the bird's still alive, so if he and Harry are satisfied—"

Her face was alarmingly still. Was this his idea of civilizing her? It seemed more like a challenge. She stared at him without speaking for long seconds. Then she said, "Truman Hall, what have you done to that shirt?"

Truman glanced down at himself. Just below the edge of his beard was a neat three-cornered tear. "By golly—"

"Go take it off and put on one of Clayton's! I'll mend that just as soon as I get a minute."

Truman nodded meekly. "Thank you, Sarah. Don't know how I come to do that." The two men disappeared into the back bedroom.

Aunt Sarah turned back to the stove. "I don't need that old fool to tell me when I've done wrong," she said after a minute, stiffly.

I didn't know how to respond. I felt my face get red.

"We do need to eat these critters," she said. "You won't go making pets out of all of them?"

"Oh, no," I said. "No."

She turned from the stove with the platter of salt pork. I took it from her and placed it on the table. Both of us were warm and red faced and glad to have Truman and Uncle Clayton return. Truman draped his torn shirt over the back of a chair. I touched it as I passed. The fabric was worn nearly as transparent as the blue bandanna I'd borrowed last night.

"I'll mend this," I said. It seemed only right; I had a feeling the shirt had been torn on my account.

Uncle Clayton bowed his head in a brief, silent grace, and I looked at his hair, lank and gray streaked with brown. Then we ate, and after the first awkward moments there was real conversation. True, it was all about farm work, just as the weekday exchanges had been. But Truman hadn't visited in a while, and the way the grass was coming along, the thin place where the beans weren't growing, the new pigpen gate, all had to be explained in expansive enough terms that I could understand them, too. Everything was work here. Everything was food and firewood and racing the summer to get both put away in time. It was a life Mother had turned her back on, by moving down the hill to West Barrett, by staking my future on an Academy education. But it was new to me, and the distraction, any distraction, was welcome.

After dinner we washed up, and I mended Truman's shirt in a neat, nearly invisible darn, as Mother had taught me. While he was changing again, Uncle Clayton harnessed Jerry and brought him to the front door. Aunt Sarah came out of the house with a covered pie carrier.

Truman climbed into the buggy and snapped his fingers to Tippy. She leaped up, looking sturdy and balanced after his awkwardness. Aunt Sarah put the carrier on the floor. "Now don't let that dog eat this!"

Tippy had indeed sniffed the plate, but all at once she stiffened and looked past us, down the lane. After a moment a buggy appeared. "As good as livin' on Main Street," Truman said, settling back against the cushion with a pleased, expectant look.

I recognized the horse now, and after a moment I could see Dr. Vesper's face.

"Well, they're all out waitin' for a man!" he cried, and pulled up close to Jerry. "Trume, you're looking almost human! Sarah, Clayton. Hey there, Harry!"

In this yard, among them all, he seemed young and

boisterous, like a classmate of mine rather than my doctor and guardian. He didn't look exactly as I'd remembered him. It hasn't been that long! I thought.

"I'm here to take you down to Barrett, Harry."

"*Really?*"

For a second he looked surprised. "Why, yes. You're to stay with the Mitchells while you take your exams."

I had hoped he was taking me away for real and always. It took me a moment to gather my thoughts. "I'll get my things."

Only then did I notice Aunt Sarah's silence. She stood very still beside Truman's buggy, her face rigidly composed.

Was I supposed to ask if I could go? My cheeks burned. To heck with that! I thought, forming the words deliberately in my mind, and I went upstairs to pack a carpetbag.

When I got into the buggy, I was at eye level with Aunt Sarah. She wore her marble look.

"I'll have her back sometime midweek," Dr. Vesper said.

"All right," said Aunt Sarah, as if it made little difference to her.

I looked over at Truman and Tippy. He had his arm around the dog. No, on that side Truman didn't have an arm.

"You go first, Andy," he said. "We don't care if we never get there."

twelve

The Mitchells lived on Barrett Main Street in a big brick house that once was white. As the paint wore away, the brick color showed through, a soft terra-cotta.

The house was as familiar to me as my own. Luke and I have been best friends since Mother first began to sew for Ida Mitchell. We were three years old, and we can't remember a time when we didn't know each other.

Still, I opened the front door a little timidly. Luke hadn't been waiting in the yard. Dr. Vesper drove off with a cheerful "Good luck!" and I was alone again.

"Hello?" I said, into the fern-filled front hallway.

Upstairs something banged, and Luke looked over the banister. Her dark braids hung past her face. "Harry! Hang on!"

She cascaded down the stairs, and I saw the exact spot, halfway down, where she remembered that things were different. She flushed and came more slowly. Is she afraid? I wondered. She looked afraid.

"Harry," she said, and stopped. She still had her mother and the big brick house, and she didn't know what to say to me. I felt sorry for her, a little.

"Hi," I said. "Were you studying?"

She nodded. "Algebra."

"I haven't even looked at it. Can we drill?"

Luke looked—what? Disappointed? "Sure," she said after a minute, leading the way upstairs.

Algebra, Latin, and history got us through the afternoon. Supper was harder. Beautiful Ida Mitchell, in the skirt and shirtwaist Mother had made her, dark hair swept up the way Mother used to wear hers, made me want to cry. I had to brace, make my words curt and few. She kept looking at me, and I could see her love and concern. I stared at my plate. I never had this problem with Aunt Sarah.

After supper we studied until Mrs. Mitchell made us go to bed. Then we laid out the corduroy-covered floor cushions I've been using since I first slept here, at age seven. I cried that first night, I remember. I was homesick, and even a hug from Mrs. Mitchell didn't help.

Now I lay in the dark with my eyes open. My heart hurt. I dug my fingers into the blanket. I always thought heartache was a figure of speech. I never realized it was literal.

"Huh!"

A hushed, gasping sound from Luke's bed. I listened. Her breath trembled. There was a tiny sniff and then another "huh!"

"Luke?"

Her breath stopped entirely for a second. Then came a big sniff, and she asked, "What?" in a steady, muffled voice.

"Are you crying?"

"No," she said, and gave another hiccuping sob.

I sat up. "What's the matter?"

"Nu-nothing."

"Oh."

I started to lie back down when Luke suddenly burst out, "Are you still my friend, Harry?" I leaned, frozen, on one elbow. "Because—you haven't said *anything* to me! I've cried every night, I feel so bad for you, and—and you just want to do algebra!"

She sat up among her tumbled white sheets. The moon was bright enough to show the dark flow of hair down her back. Tears glittered on her cheeks.

"Luke . . ." It's too much if *I* have to comfort *her*, I thought. It's too much.

"I'm sorry," Luke whispered. "I meant—I wasn't going to—" She threw herself facedown on the pillow. Her whole body shook with crying, and before I thought, I was on the bed putting my arms around her.

As soon as I touched her, I started to cry, too. I knew how bad she felt for me, and I knew that I felt so much worse than she could guess, and that she was full of relief not to be in my shoes and was ashamed. It was all one pain, and we cried into the same pillow with our arms around each other.

When we finally stopped, we both needed handkerchiefs—two each in fact because Luke uses dainty linen squares. They made me think of Truman's bandanna. With a hiccup I said, "My uncle—"

"Wait," Luke said. She went to her door and listened a moment. "Be right back."

It was several minutes before she returned and closed the door behind her. Something clinked when she sat down on the bed. In the moonlight I made out a tray, glasses, and a decanter.

"Mother's cherry cordial," she said. I heard the sound of pouring, and then she pushed a glass into my hands. "It's very res-restorative."

I sipped. The cordial was sweet in my mouth and hot all the way down to my stomach, and only after I'd swallowed did I taste the cherries. "It's good."

"Is it?" Luke took a swallow and choked. "Well! Kill or cure!" We sat shoulder to shoulder, leaning against the wall with our legs stretched across the bed, and I told her nearly everything, beginning with the house and ending with the colt.

"I have to train him. It's the only way I can keep coming to school—if I can even afford it. But he's afraid of *hens*, Luke!"

"What if you meet an automobile?" Luke whispered.

Then I'll see Mother sooner than I expected! I thought. Taking a moment to steady myself, I said it out loud. Luke laughed, and sniffed, and sloshed more cordial into our glasses.

The tray, glasses, and cordial were gone when we awoke. We went apprehensively to breakfast, but Mrs. Mitchell only said, "Another time, girls, get up and make cocoa."

We went out onto the sunny street. We were both nervous about exams, but beyond that I dreaded walking through the Academy door. The last place I was happy was in Miss Spencer's classroom, in the moments before Reverend Astley walked in.

But we met Billy halfway there, and then some others. After the first moments, when each person flushed and looked down and my insides burned, they were glad to see me, full of questions that skirted around Mother and centered on my new life and future. There were exams to worry about, tips to exchange, and all the while Luke stood shoulder to shoulder with me. We'd shared all that could be shared. I felt strengthened.

The two days passed quickly. When Latin and algebra stared me in the face, I had to forget everything else. The rest of the time Luke and I were together. We walked by the river. We climbed trees. We cleaned an unused stall in the Mitchells' stable and mended the fence of the second paddock, so the colt would have somewhere to stay while I was at school.

We were surrounded by other projects that had started with a bang: a board across the crotch of a maple that was going to be our tree house, a wavering line of stones and rough earth that was our rock garden. I could see the paddock staying empty, the boards falling down again.

But if the colt never got here, then I wouldn't, and when would I see Luke? I pounded nails fiercely and tried to believe we weren't just playing.

After the last exam we walked to the graveyard. I wasn't prepared for the rectangle of bare earth, the threads of sprouting grass. It had not been very long, not as long as it felt. No one had carved the final date after Mother's name. Whose job was it to hire that done? I wondered. Beneath my father's name—*"Walter Gibson, 1873–1899"*—hers looked unfinished, as if no one cared.

I felt a hot rush of tears coming and looked quickly away. The nearest row of gravestones caught my eye. They were all Gibsons, like me: *"Melinda, wife of David Gibson, 1843–1873. David Gibson, 1842–1876. Edward, 1867–1890. Lettice, 1870–1892. Violet Anne, 1871–1895."*

"Who are they?" Luke asked.

I shook my head. "David and Melinda—they might be my grandparents."

Luke counted on her fingers. "They all died young. Lettice was only twenty-two."

"I don't know anything about them," I said.

Luke glanced at me curiously but didn't say anything.

It had always been a given that I had no family but Mother, orphaned in a fever epidemic, and Aunt Sarah, who hated us. The family was here apparently. The dates, the names, the stones began to weigh on my heart like gray storm clouds. "Let's go!"

When dusk fell that evening, we were in a tree again. We could see Mrs. Mitchell, a white blur in the front yard, weeding her flowers. The window of Mr. Mitchell's study glowed yellow. We listened to the birds and frogs and the sound of an approaching buggy.

It stopped at the front gate. Mrs. Mitchell went to the fence.

"Hello, Ida," Dr. Vesper said. He sounded tired. " 'Fraid I can't get Harry up the hill tomorrow. Spent all day delivering a baby—"

Did he deliver *me*? I wondered. He'd know if I came too early. I imagined asking him. I couldn't imagine asking him.

"Doesn't matter," Mrs. Mitchell was saying. "She's perfectly welcome to stay here."

Dr. Vesper hesitated. "Thing is, I don't want to get her in Dutch with Sarah."

"I see. Then I'll drive her up. We can take a picnic."

"I appreciate—whoa!" The hungry horse had made a

move toward home. "She talk to you any, Ida? She was kind of mum with me on the way down."

"She's talked with Lu," Mrs. Mitchell said. "I've tried not to interfere. Nothing but time can heal Harriet, but Lu's been good for her. They'll remember this time together all their lives, I think."

Dr. Vesper made a grumbling sound. "That doesn't tell me what's going on up there." He leaned out of the buggy, pitched his voice low, and for a few moments the words didn't reach us. Then he sat up. "Tell her I'll be up soon and we'll have a business session. And will you stop by Althea Brand's on your way up? Thanks."

He drove up the street. Luke and I slipped quietly down the tree and through the back door, ready to be told the news.

It seemed a pleasant plan: a drive behind Tulip, a roadside picnic. It was only after we'd blown out the lamp and stopped talking that I began to see it happen: Luke and her mother meeting a car, the horse running down that steep hill.

That won't happen. Tulip's very calm.

But the buggy kept tipping over. Both of them were killed. Luke was killed. Her mother was killed. Always I was the one left alive.

It was my turn to stifle ragged breath and try to keep from sniffing.

In a few minutes Luke said, "Harry?"

"What if you meet a car?" I sobbed. "What if your mother dies, too?"

Luke started crying instantly. "I know, I know. I keep thinking that—"

We were crying too hard to stop ourselves. Luke got

out of bed and took my hand. We went downstairs into the parlor, where Mrs. Mitchell was just rising, alarmed.

She put her arms around us and drew us down on the sofa. "Oh, babies," she said. "Oh, babies."

"What's the matter?" I hadn't even noticed Mr. Mitchell in his chair.

When we could make ourselves understood, when we'd been given handkerchiefs and had blown our noses and only sobbed from reflex, we all sat on the sofa together. Luke's father hugged her, and Mrs. Mitchell kept her arms around me. Patiently they explained how Tulip had been taught not to fear automobiles. They had a Model T of their own and had spent hours on the job.

"I was just as afraid as you girls are," Mrs. Mitchell said, "but Tulip is well trained now, and he's the calmest animal God ever put breath in."

"But you can't guarantee," I said.

"No," Mr. Mitchell said. "Nothing's guaranteed. But we've done everything we could."

We went to the kitchen, all four of us, and made cocoa. Then Mrs. Mitchell settled us back in bed, as if we were indeed babies. Tomorrow I'd be back on the hill, a grown-up among grown-ups.

I wished I could always stay here.

thirteen

Before Mr Mitchell went to his office, he took us out to the pasture. Tulip crunched oats, and Mr. Mitchell drove the Ford in circles around him. Tulip tossed his head, looking annoyed.

"You'll have to train your colt this way," Luke said, turning to me with wide, serious eyes. "Bring him down here, and Papa will help."

But how would I get him down, I wondered, when I couldn't lead him past a scratching hen? It was going to take so much work. I felt a stir of impatience to get home and get started.

We reached West Barrett just as the mill stopped for lunch. I saw Luke's mother struggle not to look at our house. Tears glittered on her lower lids.

Althea popped out the door as soon as we stopped. "Harriet!" She squeezed my hands gently, with a quick look at my fingers. It took me a moment to remember how I'd stabbed them on the screen.

The kettle whistled on the stove, and the green teapot stood ready on the table. Althea poured boiling water over the tea leaves. Then she said, "Ladies, I need to show Harriet something. Will you excuse us a moment?"

She led me upstairs and opened the door of her spare bedroom.

Althea's spare room had been very spare: one old bedstead, one thin rug, one washstand. Now the bed was crowded with books, rolls of fabric, framed prints. Here were the pitcher we put wildflowers in and, next to that, our rotary eggbeater.

"Two o'clock every single morning," Althea said, "I sit straight up and think, 'But we never took *that*! She'll need such and so.' And along toward daybreak I walk up and get it. I told Andy Vesper, we didn't have time to think before, any of us, but I just couldn't square it with my conscience if I didn't rescue the things Harriet ought to have."

I touched the pitcher. Just a few weeks ago Mother had filled it with lilacs. "Thank you," I whispered.

"I thought it'd be just you and Andy," Althea said, "and more room in the buggy. But you take what you want right now, and the rest'll be here."

I looked at her, dried up like a raisin in her patched old dress. I wanted to say something, but I didn't know the words. I felt . . . *proud* of her, but a girl can't say she's proud of an old woman. I reached for her hand again and felt her hard old fingers squeeze mine.

After tea I made my choices. Luke came up with me, looking sober. She would be thinking of the brick house on Main Street, with its rugs and ferns, its furniture and knickknacks. A house seemed permanent, but here was our house turned into a forlorn pile of objects. That could happen to anyone.

I took my rug, my quilt, a small pile of books, and the flower pitcher. Later we passed a rosebush blooming beside the road. I filled the pitcher with white roses, nourishing them with lemonade from our jug.

Tulip was a slow horse, and Mrs. Mitchell didn't hurry him. We stopped in one of the blackberry pastures and lingered over our picnic. Still, we got closer and closer, my stomach got tighter and tighter, and then we arrived.

I heard the clink of hoes on stone and found them in the potato patch. Aunt Sarah came toiling up the hill, like a potato herself in brown gingham. I looked at Mrs. Mitchell, light, slender, and graceful in dotted Swiss. She looked like Mother. There would be trouble.

She shook Aunt Sarah's hand. "Mrs. Hall, I'm Ida Mitchell. Harriet's mother was my dear friend. And this is my daughter, Lucretia, who is Harriet's dear friend."

Aunt Sarah stiffened, and I knew why. Behind her words Mrs. Mitchell was saying, clear as paint: This girl is not alone in the world. I take an interest in her.

Aunt Sarah didn't speak. Mrs. Mitchell went on. "My husband and I wanted you to know that we'll help when Harriet decides how to manage school. The horse can stay with us during the day, and Harriet herself can stay anytime she needs to."

"The horse isn't trained," Aunt Sarah said.

"He will be. Also, we spend two weeks at the seashore in August, and we'd like Harriet to join us this year."

Luke and I looked at each other. We'd heard nothing of this.

Aunt Sarah seemed to swell on one of her long breaths.

"Go help Harriet bring in her things, Lu," Mrs. Mitchell said. Color was beginning to glow on her cheekbones. I strained to hear as Luke and I collected my belongings and went inside.

I could make out nothing until I'd reached my room. Luke stopped at the top of the stairs, but I rushed to the window. They were right below me, and their voices came clearly.

"I'm to have the care and feeding of this child, but apparently I have no say in what happens to her!"

"Of course you have a say in what happens to her. But at her age and in her situation she must have a great deal to say for herself, especially about her education."

"I know what education did for her mother!" Aunt Sarah said.

I turned quickly from the window. Luke mustn't hear this. "What do you think?" I asked in as carrying a voice as I could manage. As I'd hoped, Aunt Sarah's voice sliced off.

"Oh, Harry, it's *awful!*" Luke looked around with tears in her eyes.

I shook out the rug beside the bed. "There! This helps, and the quilt." I folded it over the back of the chair. "And the roses, of course." I put them on the windowsill, and glanced down. Aunt Sarah and Mrs. Mitchell had stepped apart from each other.

Mrs. Mitchell called, "Lu! I'm ready to go!"

Luke said, "We've got to get you out of here!"

When the rattle of the buggy wheels had died away, the place seemed still and empty. The afternoon was hot. Aunt Sarah had gone back to hoeing, and I was alone in the kitchen.

My footsteps were loud as I crossed to the pantry. I lifted the lid of the spring box and took out the dripping pitcher of buttermilk. I drank down a glass of it, rinsed the glass, dried it, and put it away. There! I'd left no trace. Nothing in this kitchen showed that I had ever been here. No task awaited my finishing, no book was left open on its face, no spot of color or life appeared; just drab cleanness and the smell of vinegar.

Vinegar Hill! I thought suddenly. That's the name for this place! It cheered me immediately, as if I'd struck a secret blow for myself. My unfinished task awaited me down in the pasture. I changed my clothes, went down, and caught him.

After Tulip the colt seemed extravagantly beautiful. His nostrils flared wide and thin like bone china teacups. His red-gold coat, with the veins close to the surface, seemed to promise a hot, sensitive nature. Mother and I had loved to look at him. He'd be just like Belle in a few years, we thought.

"Right now I'd be happy if you were a little more like Tulip," I told him. He snorted at hens. He shied violently at the currant bushes, which I could understand, because they had been veiled in white netting. But being terrified of an apple crate and the hay rake made no sense at all. I couldn't make myself say "whoa," and praise him when he balked and bugged his eyes, not when, from the potato patch, Aunt Sarah could see it all.

"Stop it!" I said sternly, and jerked the rope. Truman's way wasn't the only way to train horses.

During supper Aunt Sarah sat ominously silent, glancing toward me from time to time and pressing her lips tightly together. She must have been brooding all afternoon, and now she was trying to keep from saying something.

I felt hollow. I've never managed not to speak unwise words when they're on the tip of my tongue. I may know better, and for a while I may be able to congratulate myself on restraint, but the words always burst forth anyway, as if holding back only gave them a bigger head of steam. I think it's that way for everyone.

Suddenly Aunt Sarah said, "Does this dear friend of your mother's have any notion of work on a farm?"

I put down my fork and sat looking at her. I wasn't going to waste my powder defending Ida Mitchell, but in fact, she knew all about farm work. I remember her saying to Mother, "From the day I weeded my first acre of potatoes I've wanted to marry a man who lived in town." She was laughing at herself because Mr. Mitchell had been a farmhand when they met. "Love is blind!" she said.

Mother didn't laugh. "No, Ida," she'd said. "Love sees truly. Anything we do for any other reason is apt to be a mistake."

"How does she know we can spare you in August?" Aunt Sarah was asking.

"Don't know why we *couldn't*," Uncle Clayton said. Aunt Sarah and I both looked at him. He looked down at his plate, but he said, "We never do need anybody besides us and Trume."

"We have extra mouths to feed!"

"I'll be very happy to do my share of the work," I said. "I didn't ask to be taken to the seashore!"

"And I didn't ask for—" She clamped her mouth shut.

I sat stiff in my chair. Next she'd say that thing about Mother, and I would have to fight.

"Can you churn?"

I almost didn't understand the question. It took me a moment to answer. "I never have."

"I'd like you to take that over for me," she said.

"All right." I had no idea what I'd agreed to, only a surging determination to do it well and thoroughly.

Aunt Sarah's hackle was slowly going down. "A half day's work is plenty. I've never believed in working youngsters too hard."

What youngsters? I wondered. She'd had no children that I'd ever heard of. How could she set herself up as an authority? But I only said, "Fine."

Uncle Clayton glanced from one to the other of us and seemed to think that the storm had blown over. He got up and went to look out the window. "Well, guess I'll cut hay tomorrow."

Aunt Sarah frowned. "That looks like mackerel sky to me."

I hated to agree with her, but it looked like mackerel sky to me, too—thin clouds laid across the blue like a fillet of fish with the flesh just pulling apart.

Uncle Clayton shook his head. " 'Twon't amount to anything," he said, and yawned. "Time for bed."

Down on Main Street Luke and I would be climbing into a tree about now, the evening just beginning. Here at Vinegar Hill we washed dishes and headed to our bedrooms as the clock struck nine. It wasn't even dark out.

I put on my nightgown and drew the rocking chair near the window, where I could look out on the barn roof and the weather vane horse striding across the dim early stars. At home nine o'clock found the sewing machine still humming. I'd be setting a hem for Mother or maybe reading aloud. No question about her character would ever have crossed my mind.

Not that I thought Mother was perfect. When you live with people, you see them scratch and hear them sniffle. You know if they swear sometimes, on running a needle into their thumbs, and then scold if you do the same. You know if they're stubborn, and if they listen to gossip, and if attention to detail might make their accounts true up.

I knew these things about Mother, but I never knew her to do anything big and wrong. Have a baby too early. Not tell that baby things she needed to know. Aunt Sarah hadn't said it again, but somehow, by not saying it, by not making me fight her, she'd caused the doubt to bite inward.

Was it true?

It couldn't be—but how could I *prove* that? "When is your birthday?" Aunt Sarah's voice nagged. "When were your parents married?"

My birthday was February 14. That much I knew. Mother and Father's wedding date was another matter. She had neither celebrated nor mourned their anniversary, just as we never visited his grave or came back here. Everything was forward with Mother, but there must be some record. A marriage certificate, perhaps. Althea and I hadn't thought to look for papers like that when we did our late-night packing. Would Dr. Vesper look before the house was sold? Or were those things already in the care of a lawyer?

All at once I remembered the wallet. I'd put it in the the bureau drawer without even looking inside. It hadn't seemed to belong to me.

I carried the candle over and looked inside the wallet. A few coins weighted the bottom. There was a folded scrap of newspaper that, flattened out, proved to be a corset advertisement. Inside it was a crumbling red clover blossom. That was all.

I put the wallet back in the drawer and picked up my candle. The light wavered across the mirror and touched the wall behind.

That's not a wall, I realized. That's a door!

How had I never seen it before? True, everything was gray in this room, and true, the door was mostly concealed by the mirror. The mirror was what usually caught my eye, because of its odd surface. But not see a door? A short little door like this, with one corner lopped off by the angle of the rafters? I've been walking around half blind, I thought.

I mapped the house in my mind. My bedroom was in the ell. Here the house was a story and a half high. The rest of the house was a full two stories, and this door must lead to those upstairs rooms.

I felt behind the bureau. No latch. I brought the candle near the wall and angled it till I could see that yes, there was a thumb latch. The bureau was in the way and I couldn't reach it.

I set the candle on the floor and crawled up onto the bureau. My own white bulk came at me in the mirror. I squeezed one leg behind the frame, groped till I found the latch, and pressed my toe into its cold, smooth groove.

The latch squeaked open. Gently I nudged the door. It swung about six inches and stopped. All I could see was darkness. I squirmed farther over, my thigh pressed hard against the mirror frame, and it creaked.

The darkness seemed to jump. I stilled my breath, listening to the silent house. No one spoke, but I could imagine Aunt Sarah lying wide eyed, waiting for the sound to repeat. I sat a long while, the mirror frame digging into my thigh.

At last I reached my foot into the dark room, found the edge of the door, and drew it toward me. When it was close enough, I shut it with my hand. I couldn't latch it. I'd have to leave it slightly ajar, and sometime tomorrow, when Aunt Sarah was outside, I'd run up here and close it.

First, though, I'd look inside.

fourteen

In the morning I learned about churning. One sat on the back porch in a rocking chair and pushed the churn, a barrel on rockers, with one's foot. One looked at the currant bushes or the maples on the hill or provided oneself with a book. A basket and half-finished gray vest showed that Aunt Sarah knitted as she sat here. There would be time to complete any number of vests.

Maybe I should learn to knit. I needed something to keep me from thinking, but whenever I tried to read, the people, even my favorite characters in my favorite books, seemed like paper dolls. Nothing was powerful enough to turn my mind from Mother.

Away on the hillside I heard the mowing machine clatter. Aunt Sarah stepped around the kitchen; bowls clinked; the oven door slammed. Then she came out to the back porch, tying on her straw hat. "Call me when it comes together. I'll be in the garden."

I waited long enough for her to get there. Then I dashed upstairs, pulled the bureau six inches out from the wall, and peeked around the edge of the open door.

The room beyond was empty. Absolutely empty.

A closet door stood open, and the closet was empty,

too, except for the bed slats leaning in one corner. No curtains, no rugs, no cobwebs, hardly any dust. Across the room was another closed door.

I stared at the wide boards crossed by sunlight, at the creamy, violet-sprigged wallpaper. I had thought these rooms would be full of furniture. Why else would the front room be given up to storage except that the upstairs rooms were full?

This room was empty but not abandoned. It had been cleaned recently and smelled of vinegar and soda. What lay beyond the closed door, so flat and bland and white? I wanted to go open it, but it seemed a long way across the room, and Aunt Sarah might come back to the house. I didn't want her to find the churn deserted. I closed the door behind the bureau but left the bureau where it was, pulled away from the wall just far enough that I could slip behind it.

Back downstairs I rocked, and rocked, and thought of Mother, and cried. Still the butter wasn't done. I rocked some more, rocked with all my might and determination, until at last the yellow grains of butter floated in the milk and it was time to call Aunt Sarah.

Even as Uncle Clayton drove back from mowing, clouds began to gather, and by late afternoon it was raining. Aunt Sarah looked dark, but Uncle Clayton seemed perfectly placid.

"First cut of hay always gets rained on," he said. "I cut that weedy spot a-purpose."

"Seems to me after forty years a man could cut hay without it getting rained on!"

Behind his magazine Uncle Clayton murmured, "You should have stopped me, dear." Then he glanced at me and looked startled. He wasn't used to having his little flings of spirit witnessed.

When the long, wet day ended and we went to bed, it was actually dark. I waited, while the rain roared off the eaves, until Aunt Sarah would surely be asleep. Then I slid behind the bureau, sheltering the candle flame with my palm, and opened the door.

Darkness doesn't scare me, but this empty room seemed too large. Shadows lay thick in the corners. There was nothing to see here. I went straight across and opened the door on the other side.

I was looking out into a hallway. Another closed door stood opposite. I moved toward it and stopped with a gasp, sensing a black chasm to my right. I turned the candle so I could see.

Stairs. Just stairs.

I opened the next door: another room, also clean, also empty. It contained two closets, one piled with wool blankets, the other bare.

The hallway made a three-sided rectangle around the stairwell. At the other end was a third door. I already knew what I would find there, an empty room.

Why would anyone do that? Why take every stick of furniture out of these unused rooms and pile it in the front parlor? That room must have been very pleasant once, with the sunny windows and the fireplace.

Of course the fewer rooms you used in a house, the less work, but then, why was it so clean up here?

The rain continued the next day, steady and gentle. I didn't churn. Churning was every third day, depending on the milk supply. Instead I swept and dusted and washed the kitchen down with vinegar. After dinner I walked over to Truman's.

My oilskin could have been longer. It kept the upper reaches dry, but water rolled down and collected in the hem of my skirt, which also gathered moisture from the grass in the lane. The fabric slapped chill against my legs.

In Truman's yard the violets bloomed, each flower beaded with raindrops. As I walked past the sagging shed and the scent of crushed gillflower rose, the feeling of belonging came over me again. It was like the line that used to run between Mother and me, diffuse now, as if the love had become a cloud I walked into. Only here. Was she here? I paused and looked around. There was nothing to see but the violets and the trees, nothing to hear but the rain, nothing to feel but cold and wet, but—but something. Something was here that belonged to me.

I knocked. Tippy barked sharply, and after a moment the door opened. "Why, Harry!" Truman slipped his suspenders up over a sleeveless undershirt. The stump of his arm was in full view. I couldn't help staring. It looked so neat, sliced off square like a piece of meat at the butcher's. Shiny-looking skin stretched across the end.

"C'mon in!" He reached for his threadbare jacket, thrown across the back of the chair. When he'd shrugged into it, he looked ordinary again, as ordinary as a man could look with a flowing yellow beard and only one arm.

"Pull a chair up to the stove and get dry," he said. "I'll make tea."

I took off my oilskin and sat down, spreading my skirt •

and looking around the room. At first glance it seemed unbelievably cluttered. There was a cot in one corner and a woodbox in another, a table, two chairs, pots and pans, a sack of onions, a coat on the floor covered with dog hair. There were books on every surface and books through the open door in the next room.

But despite the clutter, the room was really simple. I never saw Truman look for anything. His hand just reached, and what he needed was right there. The canister. The teapot. The potholder—

Mother, I thought suddenly. It was as if I'd caught sight of . . . not her but something that belonged to her. What was it? Not the pans. Not—

"The curtains!"

"What about 'em?" A cloud of steam masked Truman's face as he poured hot water into the teapot.

"Those were here!" I said. "Weren't they? Didn't Mother make those?" They were white, with a strip of bright calico sewn across the bottom. Wasn't there a dress of that fabric?

"Yup, those were hers." Truman looked around. "Not much else. The cookstove. We figured it didn't make sense, her haulin' this stove downhill and me buyin' one and haulin' it up. So we come to terms."

That was after my father died, when Mother must have felt just the way I did now. How did she bear it? I wondered. I never knew how much grief hurt, so I never knew to ask her.

"How—how *was* she? After he died?"

Truman considered me, his fingers twisting a small section of beard into a spike. "I don't s'pose she put you down for three days," he said at last. "And you were a pretty hefty package about then, big two-year-old girl. But she held on to you, and that kept back the worst of it, I guess."

I knew what the worst of it felt like. It hurt, really hurt, in your body. Would it help having someone to hold?

Truman poured tea into the two tin cups. I wrapped my hands around mine and put it down in a hurry. Hot!

"So, Harry," Truman said, "come to visit your bird?"

I'd actually forgotten my gray rooster, dearest thing in life to me when I was carrying him down the road. "No, I'm here to tell you that haying's started." That was the errand I'd been charged with when I'd said where I was going.

Truman looked out at the dripping eaves. "Clayton's cut the weed field. What'd Sarah say?"

" 'After forty years I'd think a man could cut hay with-*out* it getting rained on!' "

"You do it well," Truman said gravely. He reached into the skillet beside him and started to break off a chunk of biscuit. Then he paused. "By golly, if Sarah was here, she'd give me a piece of her mind! Excuse me."

"I was wondering how you cut bread."

"Same way I do a lot of things. I don't." He finished breaking the biscuit and handed it to me. "I generally dump the jam on a plate and dip into it. That suit you?"

"Why don't I spread it for us?" I said, spotting a knife on the table. Everything was clean. How did he wash his dishes? I wondered.

He settled back in his chair, stretching his long legs, and watched me spread the jam. "You're like your mother," he said after a minute.

"I am? How?"

He shrugged. "Manners, I guess. Kind manners."

"Am I like my father, too?"

"Oh, you're a Gibson, all right! You've got the chin!"

I put my hand up to hide it. "You mean, like *Aunt Sarah*?"

He smiled, the slow narrowing and arching of his eyes that reminded me of the years he'd spent outdoors, marching and fighting. "Just like," he said. "You look just like she did at the same age."

"You knew her then?"

"Oh, yes! Known Sarah since before she was born. The Gibsons—the old folks—wa'n't too very much older than me." He took a cautious sip of tea, eyes focused on something far away. "The old folks! Seems funny to call 'em that. They never did get old."

"My grandparents?" He nodded. "What happened to them?"

"What happened?" He looked down, and the bushy shelves of his brows hid his eyes from me. "They died, Harry. Awful lot of consumption on this hill, back when it was full of farms. I guess maybe that's died, too. Hope it has."

I tried to remember the dates on the gravestones, to make a story out of what he was telling me, but the numbers wouldn't come back. "How old were the children—I mean, my aunts and uncles? When their parents died?"

"Sarah, she was about fourteen when she was left to mother the rest of 'em. Your father was a baby."

My age almost. Only one year older. That girl who became Aunt Sarah must have felt the same way I did, the same way Mother did when my father died. She must have held on to baby Walter the way Mother held on to me, the way I would hold on to somebody, if there were anyone to hold.

Then why wasn't she nicer? Why didn't she show a little kindness?

Truman sighed aloud, like a word, and rubbed his big hand down his face. "We was proud of her. She raised all four of 'em, even after she buried her dad. I remember when that house was full of young folks. They'd have dancin' in the kitchen most Saturday nights. . . . I was quite a bit older, but that didn't stop me courtin'. But Sarah had those kids to raise, and Clayt had two arms."

He'd wanted to *marry* Aunt Sarah?

He sat with his chin on his chest for a minute and then took a big swig of tea. That was how the beard got stained, I noticed. "And then they started dyin'," he said. "Get into their twenties, they'd get that cough. Sarah fought it, every time. She was bound and determined, but you can't beat it. Hard times. Hard times. I don't know how she stood it. This arm of mine is kid stuff compared to that."

The empty rooms were their rooms. Of course. "What about my father?"

"He was sick already when he met your mother, though Sarah wouldn't see it. He knew what he had coming to him, and he told your mother, but he couldn't scare her off." Truman gazed past the stove. After a while his chest heaved, as if to push off sorrow. "All over now. They're together."

And I'm alone.

Truman said, "But you've heard this all a hundred times."

I'd never heard it once. Oh, I knew Aunt Sarah had raised Father, and I knew what he'd died of. But Mother didn't tell her life as a story. I knew the events, but not the details, not the flow of one thing into another. The fever epidemic, the orphanage, school and love and widowhood—I knew they'd all happened, but Mother didn't look back, so I didn't either. I felt ashamed of my ignorance.

We sat silent. Outside, the drips slowed, and a breeze stirred the wet leaves. Of course Aunt Sarah hated Mother, I thought. She took away baby Walter. Mother might have shared, but Aunt Sarah never would have. It was all or nothing with her.

"So why is the house like that?" I asked. "Why are those rooms empty, and why is everything crowded into the front parlor?"

"Had some good times in that parlor," Truman said musingly. "But y'see, Harry, Sarah had to go on living there after all that happened. She had to manage some way." He glanced down at himself. "It's like this arm. Wa'n't hurt all that bad, but if they hadn't cut it off, 'twould have gone black, and the black would have spread into me, and I wouldn't be here."

"Oh." I was trying to see how Truman's arm and the house at Vinegar Hill went together. Cleaning out those rooms, where maybe they'd died, filling with furniture the room where they'd had good times together—was that like cutting off an arm with gangrene? What if I'd had to live in the house where Mother and I lived and where she died? What would I have done with her bedroom? Maybe rearranging the house was the closest Aunt Sarah could come to moving.

117

Truman gazed at the front of the stove as if it were a window. "Nothin's come out the way we thought it would. Here we thought that farm wouldn't be big enough to support 'em all, and maybe one of 'em'd want this place, and who else could they buy a little land from . . . and now the ridge is empty, and Clayt cuttin' back a little every year. He ain't a spring chicken, Clayt, for all he was the baby of the family."

"That's why Aunt Sarah hated Mother," I said. "She took my father away from the farm."

Truman shook his head, not disagreeing, just shaking his head at life. "That's about a tenth of it, Harry. Your mother was—well, you know what she was, and Sarah—Sarah ought to have had more scope. Ought to have gone to the Academy, and I s'pose Dave would have sent her if Melinda'd lived. She has great abilities, Sarah does, and we've all benefited from 'em, but it's been a narrow life, no denying that."

"I . . . see."

"Well, you don't see, Harry, but in time you will. You make sure you get your schoolin'. Sarah doesn't know what she missed—well, she does and she doesn't. But she played the hand she was dealt, like you're doin' now."

The hand I played was the Academy, the colt, my strength, and my sorrow: Mother's love within me. All this new knowledge was like another card I'd drawn from the deck. It changed everything, but for the moment I couldn't see how. "I should go," I said after a few minutes.

"Tell Clayton I'll be over."

* * *

The rain had given way to heavy mist. I walked slowly along the road, listening to drips and loud birdsong. Bright pink worms stretched and contracted themselves between the ruts. I saw a robin snatch one and fly away.

So Aunt Sarah was an orphan. Like Mother. Like Father. I come from a long line of orphans.

Everyone's an orphan, if they live long enough. But not everyone is orphaned young.

But Mother was happy. I knew now that she was happy on purpose, with sorrow in the past and sorrow sure to come, in debt, with a bad heart. *I* made her happy. She always made sure I knew that.

Before me, Father. Before Father, her school, her friends.

What's going to make you happy, Harry? I could be an orphan like Mother or an orphan like Aunt Sarah.

"But that's not fair!" I said out loud. Aunt Sarah must have been splendid. She raised them all, and Truman wanted to marry her—and then they died.

Just for a moment I felt bitterly ashamed. All I had done was hate her. When I said, "You want me to die," when she turned to me, blotched and still, she must have felt as if she'd been stabbed in the heart. "I'm sorry," I whispered.

She did try to kill my rooster. She did say those terrible things.

Still, pain could twist people. I'd felt it inside myself, mean and sour. Mother must have known that about Aunt Sarah, but she also knew that Aunt Sarah had raised my father, made a good man of him. Sending me here, she sent me back to good as well as bad.

I reached the pasture gate and paused, looking across the hills. Somewhere down there West Barrett nestled among the trees, with the sawmill humming at its heart and no view at all. I would have missed this place. But in all those years, Mother came up again only as far as the blackberry pastures.

I heard a step and felt the colt's warm breath on my cheek. "Hello, Kid." I rubbed his hot, wet neck, and he pressed against my hand, tossing his head and grimacing.

Here was *my* baby. He'd been left to me as I'd been left to Mother, and baby Walter—my father—had been left to Aunt Sarah. I crawled between the bars, struggling against my wet skirt and oilskins, and put my arms around his neck.

He tried to rub his body along me. He must itch from the rain. "Hold still!" I moved along with him, hugging the muscular neck as it tossed, but then his shoulder pushed, my heel caught in a rut, and I sat down hard.

Legs; big, smooth joints; surprised, innocent face. Sweet breath clouded around me.

"Yeah, how *did* I get down here?" I clambered back; through the gate and leaned there, scraping mud off the back of my skirt with a flat stick. "No, I won't scratch you anymore!"

The colt heaved a sigh, gazing across the hillside. Lid and lashes folded close over his eye, like calyx over bud. His breath and his warm, wet smell made an atmosphere around us. I breathed it, remembering his birth, remembering Belle's deep, soft-voiced whinny to him, remembering Mother's delight in the new little creature, and how everything about him had pointed us toward the future, when I was grown, when I was in school.

I hope I *can* train you, I thought. Everything had changed, but the future, the colt giving me independence, could still come true. If I could make it.

When I walked into the kitchen, Aunt Sarah said, "What did you do, sit down and make mud pies?"

"I—" I bit back a sharp answer. She brought the tin bathtub in from the back room and began to draw steaming water from the tank beside the stove.

"Get out of your wet things and into that tub. Your uncle's gone to town with the butter, so have a good long soak and get warm all the way through."

She turned back to her rolling pin. I peeled off my clothes, folded myself under the water, and gazed around the kitchen. Its very size made it ugly, and the snuff-colored wainscoting and the vinegar smell.

But scent it with mulling cider, fill it with young people, color Truman's beard brown, straighten Uncle Clayton's shoulders, and set them dancing . . .

"Who made the music?"

She turned her head. "What?"

"Tru—Uncle Truman said you had dances. Who made the music?"

She turned back to her piecrust. *Squeak, squeak* went the rolling pin. "I did."

I stared. As if she could feel my eyes, she said, "I had my father's fiddle. He taught me to play."

"But then you could never dance!" Not that I could imagine her dancing, but Truman had been courting her,

121

and Uncle Clayton, too. Did that happen while she had a fiddle tucked under her chin?

"I wasn't much for dancing."

No, I could see that. Aunt Sarah played the tune, and everyone else danced to it.

fifteen

The next morning the sun came out, and in the afternoon Uncle Clayton cut hay.

Big white clouds sprang up by the following noon. I watched them while I churned. At dinner Uncle Clayton glanced at the clouds only when Aunt Sarah's back was turned. His eyebrows worked like the brows of a worried dog. I didn't think, I'll tell Mother. I'd gotten over doing that. But without the words to choose for her, it seemed as if I missed half of what I was seeing. My mind felt like Truman's hand: mateless, distorted.

I could write her a letter, I thought, and that seemed so close to crazy that I went right out to catch the colt.

There was no reason for him to want to close his mouth around a piece of metal, no way for me to explain why he should. Reaching for a nose grown high as a giraffe's, prying open clenched teeth, listening to the grating of a snaffle being gnawed, I kept myself in the here and now.

As I turned the colt loose, Truman arrived. Uncle Clayton caught Whitey and hitched him to the rake. Aunt Sarah stepped out of the house, tying on her hat. Her sleeves were rolled up, showing her muscled arms. She climbed onto the rake and drove away up the hill. Uncle

Clayton hitched the team to the wagon, and Truman, having put Jerry in a stall, brought two hay forks from the barn.

"Can't I help, too?"

Uncle Clayton glanced up the hill, where the rake had begun to clack. He opened his mouth, and it stayed open.

"Grab another fork," Truman said.

We rode out on the bumpy wagon to where Aunt Sarah had begun raking the hay into rows. There Uncle Clayton showed me how to roll each row into a tumble. He made the fork look intelligent, turning this way and that as if it could feel the hay and never wasting a motion. His tumbles were smooth and lifted neatly onto the wagon. Mine looked like crow's nests, and hay cascaded onto the ground when I lifted one.

Aunt Sarah drove the rake past and pulled up just above me. I struggled without looking up, waiting for her to send me back to the house and more empty hours.

"It's like kneading bread," she said. *"Fold* it."

"Oh." It didn't make sense, but nothing I was trying made sense either. I tried folding, and most of my small, shaggy tumble made it onto the wagon.

Truman had stayed up there. By wrapping his wrist around the handle, and bracing the handle against his shoulder, he could use a pitchfork. As we put the hay up, he placed it where he wanted it, trod on it a few times, and turned for the next forkful, eventually building a load as flat and firm as a mattress.

The sun beat on our backs, and then abruptly the world went dark and cool. We looked at the sky and worked faster. The rake clacked ahead, behind, above us, as Aunt Sarah circled the hillside.

Sweat stung my eyes. My hands were starting to blister. But I noticed suddenly that my chest didn't hurt. Quickly I turned my thoughts away, to the smooth ash handle of the fork, to the black snake that whipped away across the stubble. But I couldn't help noticing that just for this moment I wasn't actually unhappy.

Aunt Sarah finished raking. She wrapped the reins so Whitey would stand and came down the hill toward us. "Shall I get up there with you, Truman? It's getting pretty high." It was getting too high for me to reach, actually, and I was hoping we'd stop soon.

"Send Harry up," Truman said.

I was expected to climb up the smooth, round side of the load, but how? What would I hold on to?

"Here." Uncle Clayton drove his pitchfork into the side of the load, so the handle stood out straight. He made a stirrup with his hand. I stepped into it and then onto the fork handle, and then Truman's hand caught mine and pulled me up.

The horses' backs were small and far away. Aunt Sarah looked like a dumpy little doll. Truman handed me his fork. "Reach down," he said, "and take the hay they fork up to you. Don't go too close to the edge now."

What was too close? I wondered. The load felt firm beneath me, but the hay was slippery. I inched to the edge, clashed my tines with Aunt Sarah's, dragged her forkful of hay to the center of the load.

"Put it on this corner," Truman said. "If we build it even, we can still get quite a bit on."

Another forkful of hay nosed toward the edge of the load. I crept toward it. Don't be such a coward! I told myself.

Suddenly I felt a hand grip the waistband of my dress. "Go on," Truman said. "I got you."

He held my dress, and I reached down again and again, learning to feel safe at the edge of the load, learning what was too far. After a while Truman let go.

"Full load," Uncle Clayton said finally, and drove the wagon down the hill. I lay on the fragrant, scratchy hay and watched the sky. Beside me Truman leaned on his elbow, chewing on a straw.

Uncle Clayton drove into the barn and helped us off the load. I watched as he reached for a thin rope hanging against the wall. He pulled it, and down from the rafters with majestic slowness swung a huge iron jaw. It hung from a heavier rope that ran through a pulley at the peak of the rafters and down again to another pulley beside the barn door. There Aunt Sarah payed it through her hands, making herself a counterweight. If she didn't do that, I realized, the jaw would fall, and crush Uncle Clayton.

When it settled on top of the load, he spread it wide. It had a tooth on each corner, like a saber-toothed tiger. Uncle Clayton sank the teeth deep into the load, stepping on each one to push it deeper.

Meanwhile Truman brought Whitey to the barn door and hooked the heavy rope into his harness. Aunt Sarah got a fork and climbed over the half wall into the haymow.

She saw me standing by the team's heads, with no idea what was going on, and hesitated. "Are you tired?"

"No." I was, but I'd never say so.

"You could help me in here. Bring a fork."

I stood with her against the back wall. Truman led

Whitey away from the barn, tightening the rope. It groaned through the pulleys, and a third of the load lifted slowly toward the ceiling, swaying and dripping hay. Its sweet green fragrance filled the air.

Then the jaw clicked onto its track, and the hay rushed above us toward the end of the barn like a ship under full sail. "Whoa!" called Uncle Clayton. He yanked the thin rope. *Whumpf,* the hay dropped into the mow. Aunt Sarah stuck her fork into the edge of the pile and glanced at me. "Do what I do," she said. I copied her, and together we pulled the hay in one mass back to the wall.

The whole process repeated twice. Then Uncle Clayton forked the remnants off the wagon and glanced at the sky. Patches of blue showed between the clouds now, and they were white, not gray. "Drink of water," he said, and crossed the yard to the house. Aunt Sarah caught up and passed him, to forestall some disaster like his drinking from the wrong pitcher.

"How you like hayin', Harry?" Truman asked, passing his gossamer-thin bandanna over his brow.

"I love it!"

Two weeks after dropping me off, Luke wrote:

> Dear Harry,
> Have you ridden him yet? I hope it's going well.
> Was your aunt mad after we left? Mama was
> so mad she *swore!* Don't let her crush your spirit,
> Harry. That's what Mama says she wants.
> Remember, we are here.
> Papa says give your colt time to see for himself
> that things won't hurt him. He says a horse

never forgets what he figures out for himself,
but things you pound into his head go right out
the other side.

I can't wait till August, can you? Hazel says
Billy misses you and carved your name in one of
their trees, but I saw him holding hands with
Mildred Dean, so I don't know. I think he likes
all girls.

Write back.

> Love,
> Luke

Write back? How could I explain that everything was
different from the way it had seemed? The empty hill
was populated with people dead and gone. They
bloomed slowly to the surface of my awareness, the way
yeast springs to life in the proofing bowl. No one had
spoken their names in years: Edward. Lettice. Violet
Anne. No one spoke of them now, except Truman once
in a while, but I knew about them. They lived inside me.

We hayed and hayed and hayed, and time slid by. I
fell into bed exhausted and woke up aching. In the morning there was churning or housework. Just after noon I
worked the colt. Then came haying and the hot sun, the
smooth-handled pitchforks, stop and start of the team,
clink of harness, Tippy's white tail waving as she hunted
mice in the weeds—sweat, chaff, headache, and the sorrow emptying out of my body. In the hayfield I felt like
a figure in a landscape painting, not like a person. It
helped.

Aunt Sarah watched me closely. "Don't run with a
fork!" she snapped when I did that. She made sure I

wore a hat. She passed second helpings of dinner before I asked. Even so, the waists of my dresses began to hang slack.

And how was the colt? What would I have written to Luke if I'd managed to answer her letter? I had ridden him—sat on him anyway—but no one saw it. He was standing beside the fence, surrounded by cows, and I just slid on. He didn't do anything, only curved his neck around to sniff my foot, and then ambled along the fence line, reaching under it to snatch bits of grass. When he turned downhill to chase a cow, I slid off.

Not much else was as easy as that. Every day he walked sleepy eyed to the gate, but as soon as he stepped over the bottom rail, his head came up, his neck stiffened, he began to bobble and step on me and look for things to shy at. Every day. The only sign of progress was that he now ignored hens.

Bridle him: the giraffe game. Saddle him: always easy. Then I would lead him behind the barn where the hay was just cut and circle him on the long rope, teaching him my language. Walk. Trot. Whoa. No. No. No.

One afternoon I led the colt to meet Truman. It was a cooler day than usual, with a light breeze stirring the leaves. The colt walked on tiptoes, flaring his nostrils. A bright patch of sunlight on the ground stopped him in his tracks. A rustle in the bushes set him trotting around me like a carousel horse. I gave him a sharp smack on the neck. "Cut it out!"

At the corner I paused, intending to wait for Truman. I'd never seen a car here, but this was the main road, and with the colt in this mood I didn't dare chance it.

He snatched at grass. "No, stand!" I brought his head

up, and he gazed off across the fields, focusing on something I couldn't see.

All at once he turned to look uphill. A bush blocked our view of the road. Is Truman coming? I wondered, when suddenly I heard *knock—knock—knock-knockknock*, a small, dense sound, very close.

That's his *heart*!

Something's going to happen! I stepped closer. "It's all right. It's Truman. It's Jerry." He ignored me, straining his ears forward, each breath deeper and quicker than the last.

Then he began to back. I went with him, close to the trampling hooves. He ducked left. I went that way, too, blocking him, moving with him. If he pulled against me in this deep a panic, he would certainly get away.

He backed, ducked right, then stopped and snorted, as loud as a locomotive's brakes. I felt a mist on my face. He bobbed his head high, low, high again, stood still, and I risked a glance over my shoulder.

At the end of the lane Truman had halted Jerry. "Hey there, young feller!" he sang out. "Hey there!"

The colt's head came down three inches. His ears swiveled forward and back, and sheepish creases appeared in his eyelids.

"There," I said. "There." I scratched his shoulder, where Belle used to scratch him as they stood under the willow tree. He scratched back. "Careful," I said. "No teeth!" When the hardness went out of his scratching, he was calm, and I led him to greet Jerry.

"I heard his heart, Truman! I *heard* it: *bump—bump— bump-bumpbump*."

"Like a pa'tridge drummin'," Truman said. "That was good, the way you handled him."

"I didn't do anything."

"That's right. You didn't yell; you didn't haul on him, or hold him too tight, or make any one of a dozen other mistakes. You kept your head."

I *did*? "Not on purpose," I said.

Truman's beard and hatbrim seemed to close toward one another, his face retreating behind them. He was grinning under all that hair, as if I'd just said something clever and important. "Maybe next time you will," he said.

I felt myself blushing and turned to the colt. His neck was low, and he stared into space, as if reliving his moment of terror. He looked exhausted. I stroked his neck. We'd been through something big together.

"He trusts you more," Truman said.

I looked down. I never wondered whether he could trust me. I was always wondering whether I could trust him.

sixteen

L ater that same afternoon, while we were in the hay-field, Dr. Vesper drove up. His lightweight buggy bobbed over the bumps. The horse stopped and perked his ears at our wagon, cheerful and idle as a man on vacation.

"Hey there, Harry! You look as lean as a wolf!"

"Hi!"

"Been an epidemic of health in Barrett, so here I am. Give you folks a hand?"

"Last load," Uncle Clayton said. "Sairy, we can get this. Why don't you two go on and have your talk?"

"Ride with me, Sarah," Dr. Vesper said. "Between us maybe we can hold this buggy down."

"I'll bring the forks," I said, and followed the buggy down the slope. I could hear my heartbeat, the way I'd heard the colt's this morning. Soon I'd know—what? Something I didn't know now. Something I didn't want to know. I looked uphill. The load of hay bulked against the sky, and the two old men looked thin, bent, and knobby. I wanted to stay with them.

In the kitchen Aunt Sarah poured three tall glasses of buttermilk, and we sat at the table. Her face was brick red and sweating evenly all over, like the glasses.

Dr. Vesper held a cigar box in front of him. He fidgeted the lid up and down, up and down.

"Well, the house is sold," he said abruptly. "Didn't fetch quite what I hoped for, but your debts are paid, Harry, and you've got seventy-eight dollars in the Barrett Savings Bank."

"Oh." I didn't seem to feel anything. Seventy-eight dollars. "Who bought it?"

"Mike Callahan, the mill foreman. He married Bridget Murphy, and they've got two little girls."

"Oh." How much did tuition at the Academy cost?

"So here's your bankbook." He opened the box and handed me the little leather book. "You need me or Sarah to sign for you if you want to withdraw any of it. And here's the bill of sale for the house, and your mother's deed, and some other papers she had. I come near throwin' this box out, but Althea said we should look in it first."

He pushed the box across the table, and my fingers closed around it. Seventy-eight dollars and a cigar box.

Dr. Vesper took a long swig of buttermilk and folded his lips in on themselves. "Harry." He hesitated. "Well, I'll just spit it out, and then I'll know how you take it, won't I? John Gale's paid your shot at the Academy— three years up front, cash on the barrel."

I saw him watching me, kind and sharp. I heard Aunt Sarah's breath draw in, swelling with some unknown emotion. I must have looked blank because he reached across, squeezed my hand, and gave it a little shake. "You're *set*, Harry! Tuition's all paid!"

"I—" My head felt perfectly empty.

He had the sense to go on talking. "John, he didn't

want me to tell you it was him. Thought you might not take it. I said the Academy'll take it, like a trout takes a fly! And I said I'd better tell you. No knowing what you might imagine otherwise. But John feels awful bad. Sold his automobile, so I hear—"

"Isn't—isn't it an awful lot of money?"

"No more 'n he can afford. He's pretty well off, John Gale. Wanted to pay it all now to make sure 'twas done, he said. Didn't want to rely on his heirs if anything should happen to him."

He glanced at Aunt Sarah. Something he'd just said was not true, and he was checking if he'd put it over on her. She stared at the tabletop.

"So I'll tell him, Harry, that you'll let him do this? You aren't offended?"

I tried to pull myself together. "Tell him—tell him thank you. I'll ... write him a letter."

"Good girl. I guess it's no more than right, though it wasn't his fault. What do you think, Sarah?" He darted the question at her like a cow-dog nipping at the heels of a bull. Don't, I thought.

She looked at him, and at me. I noticed the fine netting of lines all over her face. "I think Harriet had better start making progress with that horse," she said, and pushed back from the table. "Doctor, will you stay to supper?"

Dr. Vesper smiled to himself and stood up. "No, thank you, Sarah. The Old Lady thought I might like to eat one meal with my knees under my own table. I was to give you a kiss, Harry. Walk me out to the buggy?"

A safe distance from the house, he puffed his breath

out through his teeth. "Phew! That went better than I expected."

"What? What did you say that wasn't true?"

He draped his arm along the buggy wheel and studied me a moment. "You won't forget how to smile up here, will you, Harry?"

My face heated. I looked down. What an awful thing to say!

"Hey!" he said gently. He reached out and squeezed my shoulder. "Are you doing all right?"

I nodded.

"It's a lonely place," he said, "when you're the only young person."

"I guess so."

"Now you're mad at me," he said, making a wry, sad face. "In answer to your question, it's all true except the part about the heirs. We decided, me and Ida Mitchell, that if 'twas all paid up front, Sarah couldn't say no. Didn't make any difference to John; he meant to pay it all anyway. Now that was clever of me, and I've known you all your life, Harry, so don't you think I could be forgiven?"

"*All* my life?" I asked. "Did you deliver me? Were you here when I was born?"

His eyebrows jumped. "No, you were in too big a hurry. Your aunt Sarah delivered you."

Aunt Sarah delivered me? The first person whose hands ever held me was *Aunt Sarah*?

"Harry!" Dr. Vesper sounded sharp. "Look at me, will you? Is it really all right? Because I have the power to make other arrangements."

The words had hardly any meaning. I felt the way I did when I had the measles, when the world went oily and things melted into one another. "Yes," I said, wanting only to make him go away.

The wagon had come down the hill, and just outside the barn door Aunt Sarah was speaking to Uncle Clayton. Her face was red; her eyes were big and hard. Truman stood a little back from them, and he looked troubled, though it was hard to tell with Truman. He looked surprised, too.

When I joined them, her silence slammed like a door, and we got to work. She kept looking at me, as if every time I put my fork into the hay I was doing something utterly and typically wrong. But I hardly felt the blow of these glances. There seemed to be a still cocoon of air around me.

We finished. She and I went inside and put supper on the table, while Uncle Clayton milked and Truman fed the pigs. We ate. No one said anything except "Pass the butter." "Pass the salt." We washed dishes, and Truman lingered in the rocker beside the woodbox, while the sky darkened. I folded the dish towel. "Good-night."

Truman stirred. "Harry," he said. His voice seemed to command attention. "Feelin' all right? You look a little peaked."

"Just . . . tired." I took the cigar box from the shelf where it had lain all evening and climbed the stairs, undressed and washed, put on my nightgown, and sat in the rocking chair beside the window, with the cigar box on my lap. I looked off at the apricot-colored sky. The weather vane horse trotted past tinted clouds. My fingers curled around the the box lid. I felt the torn paper seal.

The house was gone, and I had seventy-eight dollars in the bank. The number made me feel poorer than when I had nothing.

There's the tuition, I tried to remember. That's richness. But everything seemed limited, boxed off and finished. Seventy-eight dollars, and whatever important papers might be in this cigar box, and that seemed the end of Mother.

I heard steps on the stairs. Aunt Sarah's head appeared above the rail. "Are you all right?" she asked, without giving the slightest evidence of caring.

"Yes."

The round head balanced there like a stone. I could hear her breathe. I looked down at my brown fingers on the lid of the cigar box.

"Don't sit up late," she said finally. The footsteps went down the stairs.

I flipped up the lid. The soft, dim light from the window showed the bankbook and a thin stack of papers. I turned them over, one by one.

Bills from the Academy and Fuller's store, stamped "Paid in Full." A bill of sale from The Estate of Ellen Gibson to Mr. Michael Callahan, for "house and two acres in West Barrett village, just east of and adjacent to Newton's sawmill." Bill of sale for same from William Gregg to Ellen Gibson, dated eleven years earlier.

The next piece of paper I almost missed—a small browned clipping from a newspaper. It announced the death of Walter Gibson, "the most recent of his family to perish from consumption. He was predeceased by his parents, his brother, and two of his sisters. He leaves a sister, Sarah Hall, a wife, the former Ellen Tate, and a daughter, Harriet. Those who knew Walter before sickness restricted his activity remember a kind and merry-hearted youth who showed great promise."

Next came a piece of paper that I never looked at because when I lifted it, underneath was Mother, smiling straight at me and looking exactly like herself.

I picked up the photograph and held it nearer the window. It was mounted on stiff cardboard, an eighth of an inch thick, with "Barrett Photographic Studio" across the bottom in swirly letters. Mother wore a dress I recognized as her second best, and she looked happy and confident. By her side, so darkly dressed that I hadn't seen him at first, stood a tall, knobby young man. Their hands were down between their two bodies, almost hidden, and wrapped around each other, into each other, as close as they could possibly get. The man's eyes were a little staring, as if he unexpectedly found himself on the brink of exhaustion.

I turned the picture over. Her handwriting on the back was as fresh as the last note she'd written me. "Our wedding day, June 30, 1896."

I knew now why Aunt Sarah hated Mother. I knew why she would make up things that weren't true. But I counted on my fingers anyway. June to mid-February. Nine months. Nine . . .

No, I'd counted June, and June was over when they married. I had to begin with July.

Eight months then. Eight.

Babies take nine months. Every baby. Nine whole months.

So?

So what?

So it was true. Aunt Sarah had told me the truth. Mother had been pregnant when she married.

I turned the picture over, and she smiled at me again. For a moment I felt the line of love from heart to heart, and then my heart squeezed tight and cut it off.

I was in this picture. I was right there, under the bodice of the pretty dress. I looked out the window. The sky was darker. The trotting horse was black.

Does this *matter*?

I knew, roughly, how babies are made. "You'll hear a lot of nonsense from other children," Mother said, "and I want you to hear the truth from me." Then she explained, and she laughed when I made a face. "I know, Harry! It's part of grown-up love, and when you're grown and in love, you'll understand."

"When you're grown and in love." Not "when you're grown and married."

But they *did* marry. They loved each other. Look at those hands.

Three years after this he died. Did she hold his hand then, as I held hers? I remembered the feel of her hand at that moment. I remembered the feel of it in my dream. I remembered the press of her wedding ring.

I don't care about this, I thought. But I felt hollow down the center of my body, down my arms and legs. When you cut a pear in half and lift out the core with a knife—that's what I felt like. Our past was shameful, and I had never known it. My life had been built on sand.

Were we ever really happy? I reached for my pillow

and sat hugging it. "Why don't we ever see Aunt Sarah?" I remember asking. "She doesn't like me," Mother had said. There was never a reason, and I never noticed that, because there *couldn't* be a reason for not liking Mother. Not a real reason.

I had been happy. I had been confident. I was the daughter of the prettiest, nicest, most loving woman in town. A few sour old ladies disliked us, but that was because we were young and loved the world and dared to show it.

All along those ladies had been right about Mother.

She was good and loving.

She broke the rules. She never told me. Our life was a lie. In every scene, when I thought I knew what was going on, she knew something else.

Did she really like blackberrying?

Did she actually like reading "Evangeline" and "Hiawatha" with me?

Did she love our house? *Did* she love our life? Was there ever, really, any *us*?

I stood up, and the window glass was right in front of my face. Out there the night was soft and black. Below me they slept, Uncle Clayton, Aunt Sarah.

I didn't want to see Aunt Sarah again.

I would walk out of the house right now. I would disappear.

But already I was exhausted, and where would I go? I didn't want to see anyone, my friends even less than Aunt Sarah.

I put my hands up to the glass and remembered hurting my fingers in my skyscraper bedroom. *"If you ever get to the city, Harry, you won't feel like a rube."*

The city. A room in a real skyscraper, high and lonely. The people below me would be as small as ants, and I wouldn't know a single one of them.

I really could go. I could sell the colt for train fare. Saddle-broken, he'd bring enough money to live on for a while. . . .

I crawled into bed and closed my eyes. Behind my lids it wasn't black and soft. It was gray, like lake water on a cloudy day. Train him. Train fare. Train . . .

Just before morning I dreamed I was riding Mother's sewing machine to New York City: *clackety-clackety-clack.*

seventeen

I t doesn't matter.

I woke up telling myself that, before I remembered what I was pushing away. I opened the cigar box and looked at their faces—hers so joyous, his weary, far-seeing. I looked at their hands.

They loved each other. It doesn't matter when I was born.

I believed it with all my conscious might, but underneath I felt the wound. It was like the time I ripped the lace on my best dress. Mother tucked the mangled part out of sight, and people were forever complimenting me on the dress, but I never felt the same about it afterward.

I couldn't seem to rock steadily that day. Churning took all morning, and in the afternoon I rested, as Aunt Sarah had wanted weeks ago.

Now she wouldn't have minded if I worked myself to death. I felt the weight of her glance when I sat down after dishes. Uncle Clayton and Truman looked curious when I stayed there, while they went off to the hayfield. Aunt Sarah bunched her mouth, as if she knew exactly what was going on.

When they were gone, I went upstairs to my hot bedroom. I looked at the smiling face of my mother, the exhausted face of my father.

You did what only married people are supposed to do. That's bad, not like killing people, but like—like keeping a dirty house. Like drinking too much. Like cheating.

Mother's face looked brave and happy. Father's looked . . .

What if she *had* trapped him? What if she'd said, "I'm going to have a baby. You have to marry me?"

What if she *did* ruin his life?

He didn't have much life left when he met her. But he could have spent it at peace with Aunt Sarah, who raised him from a baby. He could have spent it in the house where he was born.

I put them away in the cigar box.

That afternoon the haying on Vinegar Hill was finished. They came in streaming sweat. The day had heated up beyond anything we'd seen yet this summer.

"It's a weather breeder," Uncle Clayton said. "I'll wait for a change before I cut the homeplace." Truman went home, expecting the haying to come to him in a few days.

But the heat increased, smothering us. A dress left on the floor formed wrinkles overnight, as sharp as if they'd been ironed into the fabric. Paper was limp. Milk soured quickly.

My attic bedroom was stifling, even after the thunderstorms that blew up each afternoon and cooled the air outside. Uncle Clayton waited for a big storm and wind to bring in fresh air. After each rain he listened, smelled, tasted the air, and shook his head.

Meanwhile we churned and washed and baked, weeded, shelled beans, canned vegetables. I presented myself for each task as it arose and was shown how to do it. We didn't talk, Aunt Sarah and I, but I knew what she was thinking. I'd overheard her tell Uncle Clayton. I know she meant me to hear; I'd never once overheard her say anything about me before, and I'm sure she said plenty.

"I'm to house this child, but nobody believes I'm fit to raise her! That folderol about John Gale's heirs! That was cooked up, so I'd have no say in what happened, and look at her now! Not a word to say to any of us. Thinks she's too good, I suppose, with all that money laid out for her!"

A murmur from Uncle Clayton.

"I raised four children! I don't think I made too bad a job of it! But the way Andy Vesper acts, you'd think I'd just gotten out of a home for the feebleminded!"

Murmur.

"Well, let her get herself down there then! Though I have yet to see an inch of progress with that horse that's eating us out of house and home—"

"That horse's too young," Uncle Clayton said. "And she is, too. Y'ought to put a stop to that, Sairy, before she breaks her neck."

"Oh, yes, and I can just see that Barrett crowd if I did! They'd probably have me in jail for cruelty!"

She was right. I was making little progress. The scenes repeated so often, they formed an eternal present. On the long rope, I tell the colt to walk. He keeps trotting. I yank the line.

Leading him, I say, "Whoa." He bobbles toward me and steps on my foot. I push him with my elbow.

Passing the new pigpen gate, he stops and snorts and backs up fast. I put my hand up to soothe him, and he bites me. I slap him.

I ought to have begun riding him. At home I would have, in the little pasture by the river. Here I didn't dare. The pigpen gate frightened him day after day, and what if I was on his back when that happened? What if we met a car, a rooster, a farm wagon, out on the road? Before that happened, I had to drill the commands into his head, so *whoa* meant "stop" every single time.

But it was hard to keep going. It was no fun for either of us, and why was I even doing it? He would fetch more money if he were trained, but did I believe I was going to sell him? Did I believe I'd run away to the city and vanish? Not really. I didn't believe anything anymore.

The second hot Thursday I was in the pasture when Truman drove up. The colt had been evading me, slipping away with sour ears whenever I got close. Now he brightened and trotted to greet Jerry. I followed.

"Hello, Harry!" Truman's beard looked limp and more tea stained than usual. Sweat trickled down his face and lost itself in the yellow-white fringe.

"Hello."

"Been expectin' you every day. I s'pose the weather's kept you home."

I nodded. My mouth felt tight and small. I snapped the rope into the colt's halter. He flicked his ears back angrily, and I felt an inner flick of anger in response.

"Been workin' him hard, Harry?"

"Not hard enough!" I pulled the colt's head away from Jerry and led him through the gate.

"Looks like you could both use a day off," Truman said when we caught up with him. "Why don't you come visit me? Haven't seen your bird in a spell."

"Maybe." Just what I need! I thought. One more person who thinks I can't train this—

Thunk! on the top of my head. Roman candles shot off behind my eyes. "Ouch! Oh!" *Clunk!* again, from behind. I saw the colt's head swinging.

"Darn you, cut it out!" I slapped his neck, as hard as I could. He flung up his head, mouth pinched tight.

"Harry!" Truman said. "He didn't do that a-purpose! He was bitin' a fly!"

"Well, it *hurt!*"

"The fly hurt him. Put him up for the day, Harry. You're in no mood to handle a horse."

"He has to learn!" Now my hand hurt, too. "I don't care if a fly does bite him; he has to behave!"

Truman started to speak and stopped. He sat looking at me from under the shelf of his brows. "Well," he said after a minute, "guess I'll take my own advice and leave you be." He flicked the reins at Jerry's rump. Jerry walked faster, a bumpy gait that seemed stiff in some joints, too loose in others, and that left me ever so slightly behind.

I had to hurry now beside the colt, who urgently wanted to keep up with Jerry. Already I felt greasy with sweat and bad inside. I had been disrespectful to an old man who loved me. Mother would be ashamed.

I'm ashamed of you, too! I retorted in my mind.

146

Even as I brushed the colt, the deerflies bit, and the bright blood welled up. I couldn't blame him for jumping and squirming.

It was the craziness I blamed him for, the frantic stamping at the lightest touch on his legs, even a housefly or a grass stem. It was the foolishness that made him jump and look resentful when I smacked and killed a fly on his flank. "You'll just have to put up with it!" I said through clenched teeth. "Other horses manage."

I clipped the long rope into the halter and unsnapped his tie rope. The colt ducked his head into my shoulder.

Automatically my hand came up to rub the glossy bulb of his ear. I hadn't done that, or scratched his neck, or hugged him in a long time. All I'd done was boss him, smack him, yank on his halter.

Had I been too harsh? It wasn't his fault he was only two. Maybe Truman was right. I would just work the colt briefly, and as soon as he did one good thing, I'd praise him and put him away.

I led him up to the flat hayfield above the barn. I could see Uncle Clayton and the team, small at the far end of the bean rows. Aunt Sarah and Truman were in the garden, Aunt Sarah like a big stump in her brown dress, Truman thin and angular as a heron. They were talking, about me, I thought. I turned to the colt.

"Walk."

He didn't budge. I waggled the buggy whip; he flattened his ears and obeyed, circling me at the end of the rope.

"Good— No!" He'd ducked his head, shaking it angrily, and now he started to trot. I pulled on the rope.

"You *walk*!" He kept trotting, the mincing jig Belle used to do when nervous, which had always given me a stitch in the side. I jerked the rope hard. "*No! Walk!*"

The colt stopped in his tracks.

"*Walk!*"

He lashed his tail, bit a fly just behind his elbow, and at last did walk. His mouth was pursed, and his eye narrow. "Good boy!" I said when he'd walked a complete circle. "Now trot!"

He shook his head heavily, on and on, trying to dislodge a fly. The deerflies favored the ears and didn't shake off easily.

"Trot!" I said again.

He stopped, rubbed his head against his foreleg, snatched a bite of grass.

"Now darn you, *trot*!" I snapped the whip.

The colt let out a deep, angry squeal, plunged into a gallop, and lashed out with both hind feet, all at once. He began to race around me, his body slanted toward the center of the circle, his head carried high like a lance. The rope pulled hard against my hand. I dropped the whip—it seemed to cling to my fingers—and grabbed the rope in both hands.

"Whoa!"

But the colt saw the team down in the bean field. The circle became a straight line as he charged toward them, and my braced feet lifted off the ground.

For a moment I was flying. Then I hit the grass and was raked across it, across the bumps and stubble. The rope slid through my hands. I couldn't seem to let go, until the knot in the end of it slid past my face, banged like a hammer at the base of my hands, and they opened.

I saw a bruised leaf of clover and a bare quarter inch of ground amid the stubble. The earth drummed, and slowly I knew that for the colt's hoofbeats.

I didn't want to move. The yellowed field spun and sank slowly, one quarter turn, another . . .

Something prickled my cheek. I lifted my head a fraction. Nothing moved on the broad grass horizon, but I heard voices.

The sun was hot on my back. I started to push myself upright. The ground burned my palms, and I fell flat.

I drew my hands toward me across the grass, palms up. I didn't dare look at them. I propped myself on my forearms, rolled over, and sat.

Far away the colt raced across the bean field. The long rope flew behind him. Dirt and bean plants erupted in the air.

Uncle Clayton strained his reins tight. His hatbrim tilted as he looked uphill.

"Harry! Harry, are you all right?"

How could I be hearing him? He was so far away.

Not him. I turned my head, slowly. It felt huge and light, as if it were made of cork.

Aunt Sarah, running, almost here. Her face was mottled, red and white. Truman struggled far behind her, the stub of his arm jerking and flapping like a broken wing.

"*Harriet!*" She fell on her knees beside me. Her breath came in great gasps. "Say something!"

She looked so strange. I turned my eyes away from her. The colt had made a spiral of broken, trampled bean plants. Now he pranced around the team. He'd tangle them in the rope. . . .

"Where are you hurt?" Her big, hot hands pressed my head. I winced as she found the places where the colt's jaw had whacked me. She passed one hand down my spine.

Truman collapsed on the grass beside us. He was pale, and his breath trembled, his hand trembled, as he gently reached for one of mine and turned it over.

It looked like raw meat.

eighteen

My stomach heaved. I ducked my head onto my knees, pressed my mouth against my skirt.

"Rope burn," Truman said.

I'd had a rope burn once. It was just a pink-glazed line across my arm. . . .

They were turning both hands over now. I heard Aunt Sarah's breath hiss through her teeth. After a moment Truman said, "Not as bad's it looks." Truman has seen people shot with cannons, I thought.

"Are you hurt anywhere else, Harriet? Look at me!"

I raised my big head. I felt dreamy somehow. I didn't want to speak. Aunt Sarah felt along my legs and arms. I stared off at the little, distant figures in the bean field.

"Well, Harry? You *satisfied*?"

I jerked all over. Truman's beard was sucked down into the hollows of his cheeks. His eyes sparked. "Y'drove that horse and drove him till you finally made him hurt you! I just hope—"

"Truman!" Aunt Sarah said, in a voice that was large and deep and soft. "That'll do! When this girl needs a scolding, I'll tend to it!" Her voice was so different it didn't seem like hers. It was changed the way Belle's voice changed when the colt was born, as if her labor had changed the shape of all her organs. I felt Aunt Sarah's hands, firm under my elbows. "Can you stand up, Harriet?" My name was musical in her mouth.

"I . . . think so."

As soon as I stood, the blood sank and throbbed in my hands. I had to hold them up in front of me, and then I couldn't help seeing.

"Close your eyes," Aunt Sarah said. "Looking makes it worse."

No. I felt better, now that I could see the skin in little crumbs and tatters, the blood trickling. This was no horror. It was like a skinned knee, only more so. A lot more so.

"Can you walk?" Her hot arm felt good around me. We stepped slowly together over the uneven ground. My legs were strong enough but seemed loosely connected. I was glad to reach the shade of the barn and sit down on a crate.

Uncle Clayton drove up, half standing on the cultivator and leaning back on the reins. The team pranced and huffed, ears flat, nostrils red. The colt trotted beside them. His rope was garlanded with bean plants, and brought along a bruised green smell.

"Whoa!" Muscle and tendon stood out on Uncle Clayton's forearms. "Harry, ye all right?"

"She's hurt her hands, Clayton," Aunt Sarah said. She was, for some reason, untying her apron.

Truman went past her, toward the team and the colt. "Don't . . ." I said.

Truman held his hand out. He looked both commanding and ridiculous, thin and old and one sided, still, straight, and calm.

The colt shuddered away from him, blew out a fluttering snort, and snatched at grass. But when Truman didn't move, his interest seemed to sharpen. He pricked his ears and pushed his muzzle toward the hand, sniffing.

Calmly Truman wrapped his fingers into the loose noseband of the halter. The hand looked huge against the colt's delicate profile, against the great porcelain nostrils and the tracery of veins in the face. The colt's eye rolled for an instant. Sinews stood out in Truman's wrist, and the colt seemed to wilt.

"Help me with the gate, Sarah?"

They hurried down the yard, the colt sidling to avoid the dragging rope. He looked small to me, weedy and undeveloped.

Uncle Clayton got off the cultivator. He looked different, too; I couldn't say how.

"I'm sorry . . . your beans."

He pushed the apology away. "Won't miss 'em. Want some water?"

I did. He reached inside the barn for the tin dipper and held it under the stream that flowed continually from the soapstone pipe into the water tub.

When he brought the water back, I almost reached for it. I would have sworn I caught myself in time, that I never even twitched, but it hurt anyway. My face heated with it. I felt sweat on my temples.

"Here." Uncle Clayton put one hand on the back of my head. With the other he held the dipper to my mouth. He tilted it gently and accurately as I drank.

I looked up at his face, closer to me than it had ever been. A spiderweb of lines surrounded his eyes: squint lines and smile lines. His mustache had a kindly sweep.

The colt began to neigh. Aunt Sarah appeared, half running and pulling Whitey behind her. He plodded, and all her hurry only stretched his neck.

"Clayton, harness this horse for me!"

I didn't like to have Uncle Clayton bossed like that. But he snapped to the task while she hurried toward the house, half running again, with an extra little skip every few steps as if she couldn't bear her own weight and slowness.

I let my head tilt back till it rested on the hot barn boards. The world had slowed down and come into unnaturally clear focus. I saw Truman coming. I saw how old he looked, how his gait was loosened.

He went into the barn, brought out the milking stool, and placed it beside my crate, arranging it with some care. Then he sat down.

"There! Floatin', Harry?"

I didn't even want to nod. "Mmm." Truman knew all about being hurt.

"You'll be all right."

Some quality in his voice made me wonder, and I found that by gently rolling my head to the side, I could see him.

He was smiling. Deep in his beard, hidden under the straw hat that had tipped down over his eyes, he undoubtedly smiled. I saw his thin chest rise and fall, the undershirt limp with heat. Short white hairs curled at the base of his throat. He looked . . . satisfied. Amused and satisfied.

154

We didn't speak. The sun pressed on our fronts, and the hot boards burned our backs. Uncle Clayton harnessed and hitched Whitey. The team ducked their heads into each other's necks and stamped at flies.

The kitchen door banged. Aunt Sarah came carrying a carpetbag and thrust it under the buggy seat. "Can you two manage here? Take care of the milk right away, Clayton, and you'll have to churn tomorrow. I don't know how long I'll be gone. Harriet, let me help you." She put her arm around me, and we went to the buggy.

I couldn't get in. Truman at least had one hand; I had none.

"I'll give you a boost," Uncle Clayton said. I was lifted from the waist, as I hadn't been lifted since I was a little girl. I bumped my elbow on a strut and fell awkwardly on the seat with my hands tucked up near my chin.

The buggy sank as Aunt Sarah climbed in. She clucked to Whitey, and he heaved himself into a trot.

I couldn't help gasping at the jolt. Aunt Sarah slowed him, and that was better, until we hit a rock. Then all the blood in my body hammered into my hands. I bit down on my lower lip. Aunt Sarah noticed even that and made Whitey walk. I held my hands up out of my lap; it seemed to keep the bumps from transmitting to them.

The main road was even rougher and did away with the floating sensation. I was right down inside my body, inside my hands and sweating brow. When I swallowed, my tongue made a sticky sound.

"Fool!" Aunt Sarah said. "Why didn't I bring some water?" She stared intently at Whitey's slow haunches. She could have picked me up and run with me faster than this.

We crawled down the fence line of the big pasture. I could see the house and barn, the bright copper spot that was the colt flashing back and forth, the little toy team and the toy old men. Watching, I forgot to hold in my gasp when we hit the next washboard on the road.

Aunt Sarah reached under the seat and pulled her carpetbag forward, without slowing the buggy. I watched her hand fumble with the catch. She felt inside and drew out a flow of white muslin: my nightgown and hers.

"Fold these—no, you can't." She looked ahead at the empty road, then dropped the reins on the dash and put her foot on them. She folded the nightgowns into a broad pillow and put it on my lap. "Rest your hands on this. It might feel better."

I made myself notice the softness of muslin on the backs of my hands, the very slight cushioning, the very slight improvement. I made myself hold my hands so blood would not spot the cloth.

We reached the tree line. Here I had first met Truman. *Ca-thlop ca-thlop*, went Whitey's big hooves. Lacy shadows slid over his back. The sight made me dizzy. I looked down. Here was my nightgown sleeve. Here was a bit of lace, a building up and crisscrossing of one single thread. Mother made that lace. With my eyes I followed every crisscross, up and down, up and down.

Out of the birches now, between the old pastures where the blackberries grew. *Ca-thlop ca-thlop* . . .

"How do you feel?"

My mind had gone broad and shallow, like water spilled on a table. "All right. All right."

Ca-thlop ca-thlop, past a farm, past the pasture where I had picnicked with Luke and her mother, past the rosebush, the white roses all turned brown with rain and heat. *Ca-thlop ca—*

PUT-put-put-put!

Whitey stopped, raised his head high, and higher. He looked like a statue carved in ivory.

Put-put-POP-put!

A car!

Whitey's sides heaved. His nostrils fluted out in wide cones with each breath. Far ahead the Model T seemed to leap and skip over the ruts, heading straight toward us. I heard a little whimper come out of my mouth, and I hid my face in Aunt Sarah's shoulder.

For a moment she was there, a warm wall. Then she was gone. The buggy jounced, creaked, and she was at Whitey's head. She gripped the reins close to the bit and forced his face toward the side of the road. "Whoa! You whoa! Stand—now shhh! Shhh!" The knuckles shone white on her big red hands. "Shhh, now!"

Whitey's breath rattled like falling hail. His hooves minced up and down. His tail swished. If he got away, there was nothing I could do to save myself, not even hang on. I looked at the ground, just three feet away. Jump! Jump now!

"Can you wave him by?"

I didn't understand. It was the same voice she was using on Whitey, mixed in with orders and hissing. One of Whitey's ears curved rigidly toward her. The other swiveled back and forth. "Harriet, can you wave him by? I can't let go—shhh! Whitey! Shhh!"

The car. Wave the car by.

The right hand hurt less than the left, but it felt heavy, stiff, and curled. The air hurt it, moving hurt it, and the

157

driver of the Ford took a long time to understand. Then he came cautiously, creeping along the very edge of the ditch. He wore goggles and a long white scarf. Between them little could be seen of his face. He seemed more like a bug than a human, but his mouth dropped open in human curiosity as he passed.

When the sounds died away, Aunt Sarah came back, keeping the reins tight and smooth. They never sagged once, even when she climbed into the buggy.

"Now walk, you old fool!" Whitey set off high headed, almost prancing. It was several yards before his body slackened and his head came down.

For the first time since the car had appeared, Aunt Sarah took her eyes off him and looked at me. She looked away again. "Did that scare you?"

I couldn't understand why she was even asking. It had panicked me, disintegrated me. I nodded, barely. She seemed to see it out the corner of her eye.

"If he saw more cars, he'd get over his foolishness."

I listened hard to the words. My hands hurt more than I'd ever known anything could hurt. Even shame didn't matter. Talk, I thought. Maybe that would help. "The Mitchells trained Tulip," I said. My tongue felt heavy, and the worlds came slowly. "They can lead him from their Model T."

"Can they?" She didn't like to hear that the Mitchells had done something clever. "That must be handy, though."

"But Tulip is the calmest horse in the world." I wished talking helped more. "Tulip could fall asleep on an active volcano, Mother used to say."

Aunt Sarah's breath made a little snort. "The opposite of your critter."

"Yes." I glanced at my hands, and every nerve in my stomach twanged. I closed my eyes.

We met no one else. The stone walls and blackberry pastures slipped by. After a time I smelled fresh pine sawdust, and the roofs of West Barrett came into view, few and small among the trees. Down, down we dipped, past the mill, past the little gray house—

My heart knocked. Our door stood open, and two small girls in grubby pinafores sat beside the step, stirring the dirt in the flower bed with spoons. Red checked curtains at the windows . . . It wasn't our house anymore. I hadn't realized it would change.

Aunt Sarah pulled up at Althea's gate. Before she had to shout, the door opened. "Morning!" Aunt Sarah called. "Has Andy Vesper been this way?"

Althea shook her head, coming slowly forward. She stared at my hands. "What on earth—"

"It's a rope burn," Aunt Sarah said, as if that were nothing much. "If you haven't seen him, we'll go on down. Do you need a drink, Harriet?"

I nodded. Without a word Althea went back into the house. The pump handle squeaked, and she came out with one of her white mugs, cracked and tea stained. Aunt Sarah said, "Would you mind standing at this horse's head while I help her drink?"

Althea went to hold Whitey. She looked small and distant. Aunt Sarah held the cup to my lips, and I drank. Water slopped up my nose.

"I'm sorry," Aunt Sarah said.

"No . . ."

Whitey snorted and shoved his head against Althea. She nearly fell.

"Whitey! Stop it!" Aunt Sarah said. "We'll be going."

Althea didn't step out of the way, didn't come to take the cup, for several seconds. "Stop back," she said when she did come. "I want to know how Harriet is."

"All right." Aunt Sarah let Whitey go.

The Old Lady was weeding her garden, out behind the Vespers' low Cape. She straightened, looked hard at our buggy, and headed at once for the house. "He's up the street. I'll telephone."

We were left alone in the hot, sunlit yard. How—

"Come in!" Mrs. Vesper shouted from the doorway, and disappeared again.

How would I get down? On elbows, on knees, with Aunt Sarah's hands around my waist. She tied Whitey to the ring in the barn wall and opened the door for me.

"Yes, it's Harry!" Mrs. Vesper shouted into the telephone mouthpiece. "What? I don't—" She turned to look at me. "Oh, my goodness! It's her hands, Andy! Get right down here!" She clashed the earpiece back on its hook. "Harry, sit down! What can I—oh!" She hurried into her pantry and came back with a sweating pitcher. "Lemonade!"

Aunt Sarah stood in the middle of the room, hands hanging at her sides. Mrs. Vesper almost knocked into her, rushing at her cupboard. "Oh! Sit down! Won't you sit down?"

Aunt Sarah sank onto a kitchen chair, obliterating it

from sight. She stared past me, past the wall, past the glass of lemonade that was put in front of her. After one quick look at her, Mrs. Vesper helped me drink.

We waited. The kitchen was dim and still. I could almost hear my hands throb.

A buggy rattled past the window, and a moment later Dr. Vesper came through the door. He looked at my hands and whistled. "What happened?"

None of us answered.

"Sarah! Snap out of it! Are you hurt, too?"

Aunt Sarah stirred and slowly turned to look at him, as if coming from a long way off. "No."

"Then tell me what happened!"

"Harriet was . . . training that horse of hers." Her voice was soft, almost too low to hear. "He . . . ran and dragged her."

"Rope burn," Dr. Vesper said as if that solved everything. "Come on in my office, and I'll patch you up."

I stood, feeling as if my legs were made of glass, and went with him into the bright little room off the kitchen. Aunt Sarah followed as far as the doorway.

He leaned over my hands, so close I could feel his breath, and looked them over methodically, section by section. "Harry," he murmured, "you've got to learn to let go!"

Aunt Sarah almost said something. I heard her breath draw in and then sigh out harmlessly.

"Well, it's not so bad but what it could be worse. Let's see what we can do."

I didn't watch. There was something wet that stung so much sweat popped out on my forehead. Later there was a dressing, and in the middle of that, while I stared intently out the window at the house next door, he suddenly pulled down on the fingertips of my left hand.

"*Aaah!*" It was a real shriek. Suddenly Aunt Sarah was right there beside me.

"Sorry," Dr. Vesper said. "But if it heals flat, it won't heal short. You'll thank me next time you play the piano."

I couldn't make even the first twitch of a smile. He finished the dressing; only the tips of my thumb and fingers showed. Then he started the other one. He was going to do it again.

"I'm going to do it again. Ready? There, was that so bad?"

Someone's hand gripped my shoulder. "Andy, don't be an idiot!" Aunt Sarah said.

"Now if you can, Sarah, I wouldn't mind you two staying until tomorrow afternoon. I can get a pretty good idea of what's going to happen by then. You can stay right here in the spare bedroom. Maybe Harry'd like to go lay down awhile?"

I nodded. My head felt huge again: big cork head. I followed Mrs. Vesper upstairs, into a hot, dim little room with two beds. Sat down. Aunt Sarah took my shoes off, and I placed myself on the pillow, hands at my sides, palms up.

I thought I didn't sleep. I thought my hands hurt too much. But after I had opened and closed my eyes a few times, it was evening.

nineteen

We dined on cottage cheese, lettuce, and cucumbers. Aunt Sarah fed me, and Dr. Vesper looked pleased with himself.

I still felt exhausted and not at all like talking. Aunt Sarah and I went up to bed early. She undressed me and put on my nightgown. I didn't mind that she saw me naked, though I turned my eyes away while she changed, in case she minded. Everything seemed strange and simple. My hands took up my whole mind and left no room for nonsense.

I slept awhile and awoke to the sound of Aunt Sarah breathing. Crickets throbbed. A horse and buggy passed.

Then downstairs something trilled loudly over and over. Feet on the stairs. Dr. Vesper said, "Yup. Yup. Oh, good golly, no! I'll be there just's quick as I can." *Bang-bang-bang* up the stairs, shuffle and mumble in the next room, *ca-rumble* down again, and a short time later the horse clopped away.

I lay sweating. My hands hurt more and more, hot, like bars of iron in the blacksmith's forge. I sat up.

"Harriet?" Aunt Sarah had never been asleep. Her voice was clear and alert.

"I'm all right. I'm . . . hot."

She got up, big and white in her nightgown, and went softly to the washstand. She poured water into the basin and gently sponged my face. The water was cool, but my face heated it quickly.

"I want to go outside." I could hear a breeze out there, ruffling the leaves. "Can I just go sit?"

She drew a long breath, the beginning of "no," but then she said, "I don't know why not." She went to our door. "Mrs. Vesper, we're going to sit outside awhile. Don't get up."

Mrs. Vesper came to her door, all her buoyant gray hair reduced to one braid down her back. "There's chairs on the side lawn. Harriet knows."

We crossed the wet grass. My nightgown trailed, getting heavier, but I couldn't hold it up. I made my way toward the faint white glow of the chairs and lowered myself cautiously onto a surface I couldn't see—wet, like the grass, cool.

My feet were cool, too, and the breeze felt cool on my face. Far to the west thunder grumbled. Lightning flashed pink in the clouds.

"Clayton'll be pleased," Aunt Sarah said.

After a moment I asked, "Why?"

"Storm at night means a change of weather. It'll be nice tomorrow." All I could see of her was the white blur of her nightgown. I should say something to keep the conversation going, but my mind felt empty. My hands lay in my lap like live coals.

Aunt Sarah sighed. "I haven't slept a night off that hill in over thirty years," she said.

Quite a while went by before I asked, "When did you?"

"When I was a youngster, we went to the fair." Her breath made the little snort that was laughter for her. "Well, I didn't sleep that night either! We all bedded down in the backs of the wagons, and when our baby wasn't crying, the next baby over was! I saw sunrise from the very start that morning!"

I asked into the soft darkness, "Who was the baby?"

She didn't answer right away. Lightning lit the bottom of the faraway clouds. "That would have been Walter," she said.

My father. Then she was my age that night, and her mother was going to die soon.

"I hope things are all right up home," she said.

"Will Tr—will Uncle Truman stay at—" I couldn't say Vinegar Hill! "Where will he sleep?"

"He likes to sleep under his own roof." Aunt Sarah sighed again. We both thought, I suppose, of the two houses on the ridge: the gray one crumbling back into the ground on the homeplace, the goldenrod-colored one at Vinegar Hill, with its furniture-crowded sitting room, its empty top floor.

"Which was your bedroom?" I asked. "When you were my age?"

Again the pause before the answer. "Oh, we were always tradin'. Later on, after I was married, things settled down . . . but we'd swap six or seven times in a year. And *fight*? My goodness! I remember lockin' Letty in the closet. She stayed in there two, three hours because Mother was working outdoors. Mother said to me, 'Sarah, suppose the house had caught fire?' And I said, 'Then I'd be rid of that little pest!' I got a lickin' for that."

She's talking like a regular person, I thought. Like

Truman, like Uncle Clayton. It made me realize that she'd always spoken proper English before this, like Mother, or Ida Mitchell. Tell me more, I wanted to say. While she'd been speaking, I was on the hill, rumpusing through the upstairs rooms with those children. When she stopped, I was in my hands again.

"Does it hurt bad?" she asked.

"Not too bad."

The wind came up in a strong, cool gust. The tree branches lifted and sighed. The night was blacker for a moment and then lit white. Thunder.

"It's a ways off," Aunt Sarah said, "but it's comin'. We'll have to go in soon. Here." Her white form lengthened out. She came behind me, and I felt her hands on my shoulders, rubbing strongly.

"Ow!"

"Too hard?" She rubbed more gently. "Funny how this helps, even when the hurt is someplace else. When Ed broke his leg, he always wanted his shoulders rubbed. His mind would go where my hands were, he said, and he'd forget the hurt."

My heart didn't hurt anymore. All I had room for was the pain in my hands. My shoulders winced under Aunt Sarah's fingers. I'd been dragged, too, and my muscles ached, but that was nothing.

Lightning traced a crooked trail across the sky. Before the thunder I asked, "How did Ed break his leg?"

"Toboggan. He had to make himself a jump, mainly because I said he shouldn't. Well, he didn't figure he had to obey his sister."

Her warm fingers kneaded, the lightning flashed, a few cold drops of rain hit us, and I wondered, What is happening? She'd never said their names before. They might never have existed. Now she couldn't stop talking about them, that young orphaned family, quarreling and laughing.

"We'd better go in," Aunt Sarah said abruptly.

We got up and hurried across the lawn, hearing the rain come down the street behind us. Drops hit my back like stones as we reached the door, soaking through the muslin nightgown. By the time we got inside, it was sheeting off the eaves, roaring all around us. The house seemed a small shell, like an overturned canoe.

"Good, you got in!" Mrs. Vesper came into the kitchen, wrapped tight in a dressing gown. She lit a lamp, opened the cupboard, and handed Aunt Sarah towels. "Suppose Andy got indoors before that hit?"

We had no way of knowing.

"Come in where it's comfortable," she said, leading the way into the sitting room. "No use pretending to sleep while this is going on." I sat on the sofa, and Aunt Sarah put a pillow in my lap for my hands to rest on. She dried my hair and shoulders. Then she sat beside me, Mrs. Vesper took the large chair opposite, and we listened to the rain. It drowned out even the thunder, but lightning lit the room two or three times a minute, and sometimes we heard its electric crack.

Eventually that passed on to the east, and the rain settled to a steady, silvery *sssh* outside the windows. We sat in the circle of the lamplight, surrounded by darkness, not speaking, not needing to . . .

"—way to greet a man!" The windows were gray with the dawn, and Dr. Vesper stood dripping in the doorway.

twenty

He looked at my hands after breakfast and seemed satisfied. "I'll look again in the afternoon, and then you can go home." I was rebandaged and set down to rest.

Mrs. Vesper washed the dishes, and Aunt Sarah dried them. Then she stepped to the door. The sky was deep blue. Raindrops sparkled on the grass, and the puddles shimmered.

"Harriet, where do your friends live? The ones who brought you home?"

"Down the street, not far." I'd been thinking about Luke this morning, wondering if I could go see her, wondering if I wanted to. Yesterday morning I didn't want to see anyone, especially a friend. That feeling was gone. I could remember it, but it seemed as if it had been someone else, and that someone else hadn't answered Luke's letter.

"Let's go visiting," Aunt Sarah said abruptly. "You feel up to a walk?"

"Yes." I felt miserable, in fact, not just my hands but my whole body. I had blotchy bruises all down my front. My arms and shoulders and back and neck ached. But they ached no matter whether I sat or stood or lay down. The only thing that helped was distraction.

Aunt Sarah looked me up and down. "I can't help that dress," she said, "but I'll do your hair again. I made a poor job of that." She was different this morning, firmer, concealing more.

We paced slowly up the street. I thought I must look strange in my crumpled, grass-stained calico, with my arms crossed in front of me and my hands bound up in white mitts. Aunt Sarah was definitely out of place. Every woman we met wore a dark skirt and white shirtwaist and had her hair swept up in an abundant-looking knot. Aunt Sarah was unmistakably of the hill farms, dressed in dirt-concealing brown from top to toe, her thin hair scraped back. She was frowning.

Why did she want to see the Mitchells? It was the last place I would have expected her to go. I wasn't afraid she'd say something awful. I had more faith in her now. But by the light of day I couldn't ask her questions the way I might have last night.

In the gardens delphiniums and roses lay on their faces in the wet grass. Broken branches littered the street. The Academy bell tower stood white and crisp against the blue sky, and the Mitchells' house seemed softer, pinker, grander than usual.

"Here," I said as Aunt Sarah was about to pass.

Her lips tightened as she looked the house over. A flush came up in her face, and I felt her expand with a long breath. Then she pushed the gate open and walked up to the front door.

She knocked. They would never hear that. This house was so large, so protected by its front hall, that they only heard the bell. Aunt Sarah might not see the bell, and we could go away.

She knocked again, and then her large red hand went to the bell handle. She gave it a firm, scornful twist. I heard the buzz deep inside the house, and footsteps. The door opened.

"Put it—" Mrs. Mitchell said, and then she stopped with her mouth open.

She was swathed in an apron, splashed from dishwashing, and her hair was up in her early-morning knot, slightly askew. Her face grew pink as she looked at Aunt Sarah, and her hands went on drying themselves mechanically. At last she glanced down at me.

"Harriet Gibson, my goodness gracious! What on earth have you done?"

"The horse got away from her," Aunt Sarah said. "May we—"

"Oh, come in, come in! Lu!"

Luke appeared from the direction of the kitchen, drying a frying pan. She dropped it. "Harry!"

"How badly— When—" We were all crowded in the hall, and Mrs. Mitchell was pushing at her hair distractedly.

"Yesterday morning," Aunt Sarah said, sounding matter-of-fact. "The young horse pulled away, and she got a rope burn. And that's why we're here. It's plain she'll never get the animal trained before school starts, and I concluded I should come talk to you."

Luke and I looked at each other.

Mrs. Mitchell seemed to marshal her forces. "Yes, I— Lu, will you take Harriet upstairs? Mrs. Hall?" Aunt Sarah followed her into the sitting room.

We started upstairs. "Harry, are you all right?" Luke whispered.

I looked down over the banister, at the black and lonely frying pan on the polished floor. "I'm— It hurts a *lot*," I said as we reached the landing. "It hurts a *lot*."

We heard Aunt Sarah's voice in the sitting room. "Come on," Luke said, and pushed open the door of her sister's room. She crossed softly to the grate in the floor. I followed and looked straight down onto Mrs. Mitchell's untidy bun.

Luke knelt. I didn't dare. My hands' helplessness seemed to uncoordinate my whole body. I stood close and heard Mrs. Mitchell say, "We wouldn't dream of taking money. Harriet eats nothing."

"I've seen her put away a man-size supper," Aunt Sarah said dryly, "but that was after haying."

"Yes, but we—" Mrs. Mitchell paused and looked up. She didn't speak, and her expression didn't change, but Luke sank back from the grate with a red face. "Come into my room," she said.

We sat on the edge of the bed, quiet for several minutes. "I never got a letter from you," Luke said finally. "Won't she let you write?"

"Of course she lets me. I just . . . didn't." Luke flushed. "I'm sorry. I felt . . . I can't explain. I . . . felt too bad."

Luke sat looking at me. At last she nodded, as if she understood. "You're here now," she said, putting her arm around me. "Tell me what happened."

"He . . . bolted." I didn't want to talk about it because I'd been abusing him, really. I made him bolt. "He dragged me, and then the rope slid through my hands, and he ran down into the bean field."

"Were they mad?"

"No. No, they were—" They were nice. All three of them. They all jumped to help me just as if I were their child.

As I was.

Why this should cause sorrow to swell in my throat I didn't know. Luke didn't ask any more questions. We sat side by side on the bed until her mother called us down.

Aunt Sarah looked— I don't know how she looked. I didn't know what to make of her expressions anymore. Mrs. Mitchell looked to her as if expecting her to speak, but she didn't.

"Harriet," Mrs. Mitchell said finally, "we've been discussing this coming school year. Would you like to stay here with us?"

Aunt Sarah stirred. That I understood. In her mind it was all settled, and what was the use of asking me? I was a child and would do what I was told.

"I . . . thank you," I said. "I'd like that very much." My voice sounded small and prim. It would have drawn a frown from Mother. She'd have wanted a bigger, warmer reaction.

"You're to bring us a dowry of butter and potatoes," Luke's mother said, with a nervous laugh. She hadn't even consulted her husband, and the interview with Aunt Sarah had rattled her. I should come to the rescue.

"But no beans," I said. "After what my horse did to that bean field, there won't be any to spare!"

That had been the right thing to say. They both smiled and relaxed a little. Inside me Mother approved. Oh, hello, Mother, I thought.

But where did I live now? Where did I belong? My

heart ached, strangely, for Vinegar Hill and the two ᴜ
men up there worrying.

Aunt Sarah had friends to visit, and I spent the day
with Luke and her mother. They'd been about to embark
on a lesson in puff pastry. The butter was on ice, and
something extraordinary had been promised Mr. Mitchell when he came home to supper, so the project could
not be put off.

I watched awhile. They were scratchy with each other,
a little more so when I left the room and went to rest on
the sofa. "I can't *do* it," Luke wailed once, and her mother's sigh carried all the way to the sitting room.

"Watch me one more time."

It was past noon by the time Luke came in with a tray
of sandwiches and lemonade. "I *hate* puff pastry. I wish
I'd never said I wanted to learn!"

"Did it come out all right?"

"Oh, *Mama* says it did! I think it looks awful!" She
took a big bite of sandwich and then looked at me, pop-
eyed, over bulging cheeks. Swallow. "Oh, Harry, you
can't eat! I forgot!" She picked up a sandwich, dripping
chicken salad, and pushed it at my lips.

"Wait. Slow down."

A bite for me, a bite for her, we worked through lunch.
Sometimes Luke mixed up the sandwiches. When she
gave me lemonade, it sloshed down my front, and we
laughed. But inside I felt hollow.

Mrs. Mitchell had gone to see her husband at his office.
We waited for her. We couldn't climb trees. We couldn't
play cards. I didn't want to walk; standing made my
hands hurt.

inally we went out to the big hammock. Luke steadied it while I got myself balanced in the middle, and then she gently pushed me. That hammock was treacherous; it could buck you off like a wild horse if you weren't careful. Now Luke kept her hand on it at all times, and we didn't speak.

The gate latch clicked. The hammock shuddered as Luke looked up. Then she ran to meet her mother, and I lay absolutely still, feeling the hammock sway. If it tipped, I would either catch myself with my hands and hurt them, or not use them and hurt the rest of me. I hardly dared roll my eyes.

Slowly Luke and her mother came into view, arms around each other's waists, heads close together. Two dark heads, two sets of dark eyes, two smiles shaped the same.

"Oh, Harry, I forgot!" Luke rushed to me. The hammock trembled and lurched, and she firmed it again. "Papa says yes, of course, and he's very happy you're coming to stay!"

Mrs. Mitchell put a hand on Luke's shoulder. "We're all happy, Harriet. My only regret is that I misjudged your aunt so badly."

"Yes. I mean, me too." I couldn't look away from her hand on Luke's shoulder, the wedding ring glittering in the sun. Luke and her mother. You must be very careful, Harry, a voice inside me said. You must never come between them.

I smiled and said the right things, and thought, I want to go home.

twenty-one

"This is your home now, Harriet," Mrs. Mitchell said, giving me a kiss at the door.

Mrs. Vesper said after the rebandaging, "You'll stop in for ginger cookies this winter just as if this was home?"

After Althea Brand had assured herself that I'd be all right and had reassessed Aunt Sarah, she told me, "Now, Harriet, this is your home, too. You come right in whenever you need to." She hugged me when we left and shook hands with Aunt Sarah.

We drove past the gray house. I turned my face away but heard the little girls' voices: "You be the driver!" "No, you! I want to be the horse!" I felt scalded all down my center.

But as we climbed above the sound of the sawmill, Whitey's head swung up and he stepped out eagerly. The sun was in our eyes, but by turning my head and squinting, I could see how fresh the grass looked, how everything sparkled.

Up the long hill between the fields, between blackberry pastures white with blossoms, through groves of birches. I didn't know the road well enough to be sure of each landmark. Three times we crested a rise and I expected to see the big pasture and the goldenrod-colored house.

But at last there it was. The air was so clear that every detail stood out, even the tiny weather vane horse silhouetted against the brilliant sky. Milking was over. The last cow lumbered through the gate and followed the rest downhill. A small, slope-shouldered figure put up the bars behind her, gazed down at the road, then turned and motioned. A second figure joined him.

"Look! There they are!" I almost pointed. One bandaged hand lifted involuntarily, and it hurt, but not as much as I'd expected.

"Now what kind of a mess do you suppose they've made of that kitchen?" Aunt Sarah asked.

As we turned into the lane, the colt saw us. He galloped up the hill, then trotted with us along the other side of the fence. His step was bouncy, and he carried his tail high. It flowed out behind him like the weather vane horse's tail.

"Not a notion in the world of the trouble he's caused," Aunt Sarah said. She almost sounded admiring.

I could hear the hens now. Tippy sat in the yard, wiggling all over and flattening her ears as we approached. Truman and Uncle Clayton seemed to hold back for a moment, as if they felt shy. But as Whitey stopped with a last *ca-thlop* and a heavy sigh, Uncle Clayton came to my side of the buggy and just stood looking at us. He seemed worn, almost transparent. His eyes shone, and I felt tears in mine.

"Harry. Sarah." His Adam's apple bobbed. "Didn't think you'd stay so long."

that. "I don't care about it," I said. "I don't mind any-more. . . ."

All at once Truman seemed to understand. His eyes widened, he drew a deep breath, and then he laid his arm along the fence rail and bowed his head on it.

When he straightened, the skin above his beard was rough and red. "Now listen to me, Harry!" His voice was lower than I'd ever heard it, almost strangled sounding. "Your mother fell in the barn the day you were born. That's why you came a little early. She never told Walter because he felt bad enough already, her doin' his chores in her condition. And she darn sure never told Sarah, for the same reason!"

"How do you know?"

"I ain't a fool, and I made Andy Vesper tell me!"

It crossed my mind that Truman might be lying. He might be telling me what I wanted to hear. But no, I could so easily check with Dr. Vesper, and anyway, it sounded right. It sounded *exactly* like Mother.

But just because it sounded right didn't mean it was right. Mother was an adult, with more sides to her than I'd ever seen. She was young, and the man she loved was going to die soon. She could have been pregnant when they married. I felt stupid now for thinking it so easily, for not thinking of other explanations, but it could still have been true, and it didn't matter.

"It was Sarah set you on that track, wa'n't it?" Truman said. "Nothing else'd start a young girl countin' on her fingers like a darned old maid, about her own mother! Well, Sarah, I've let you go your length, but you get a piece of my mind before you're too many minutes older!" He swung away from the fence.

"No!"

He looked back at me. His eyes blazed, and for the first time I could envision Truman going into battle. But not now. Not against Aunt Sarah, whom he'd loved, one way and another, all her life.

"It's my fight," I said. "I'll handle it. Anyway, I already didn't care, even before you told me. I think—" It was too complicated to say; my mind and heart were too full. "I don't care," I said again.

"*I* care!"

"Thank you," I said. "But I'll handle it."

Our eyes locked on each other for several more seconds. Then Truman turned away and kicked a pebble, hard. It hit the side of the barn and ricocheted off. "All right! Have it your way! By golly, Harry, you get stubborn from both sides of the family, don't you?"

"I suppose."

Truman ducked his head and laughed shortly. "Ordinarily I wouldn't recommend gettin' dragged by a horse. But it seems to have served you well."

"Served me right!"

"We all make mistakes," Truman said. He let out a sharp sigh that seemed to carry off the rest of his anger. "You know, if you'll let him, Clayton'll take your youngster in hand. He ain't what you'd call masterful, but Clayt can get a horse to see things his way. And I hear there's no hurry now."

"No."

He shook his head in a wondering way, leaned his elbows on the rail again, and gazed off at the pasture and the blue hills.

The colt nudged him and, getting no response, wandered downhill, snatching a bite of grass here and there. All at once he bucked and squealed and galloped menacingly at a cow.

"Well," Truman said, "long as you're all right, Harry."

"Truman!" Aunt Sarah called from the front step. "Supper's about ready, and I want Harriet to rest!"

"Course, your troubles ain't over," Truman said as we turned toward the house. "You're closer'n two spoons right now, but she'll always know what's best, Sarah will. Unless you plan on cavin' in to her, sometimes you'll have to fight."

"I know."

"Next time it comes up," he said, "I think you ought to tell her."

"You mean . . . ?"

"What I just told you. And it'll come up again, make no mistake. Sarah never quits, and she never uses a popgun if she's got a cannon handy. When she throws that at you again, you ought to tell her the truth. Can't hurt Walter anymore, and I think you owe it to her, Harry. She ought to start thinkin' better of 'em. She ought to have that comfort."

It was like starting over as a baby, eating supper with no hands, except as a baby I probably didn't mind helplessness and things dribbling down my chin. Aunt Sarah was deft, and when needed, she chased the dribbles rapidly with a spoon, the way mothers do. It made me cross, though, and it would be this way for at least a week. Dr. Vesper insisted on absolute cleanliness, and he'd swaddled my hands so I couldn't be tempted to use them.

"I'll start hayin' the homeplace tomorrow," Uncle

Clayton remarked over his tea. He glanced out the window at a tiny puff of cloud, golden with the last rays of sun. "Guess you won't be able to help us, Harry."

"Ride over and visit anyway," Truman said.

"Tomorrow I have to churn," I said. "I can still churn."

"Tomorrow you have to *rest*," Aunt Sarah said, wiping my chin with a damp cloth. I glanced at Truman and away, before the sparkle in his eyes could make me smile. I *would* churn. I'd sit in the rocker before she even poured the cream, and she'd say, "All right, a few minutes then," and I'd have my own way. I did know how to get around Aunt Sarah.

A wide yawn interrupted my thoughts. Without hands I couldn't hide it, and a moment later I yawned again. "Better say good-night," Aunt Sarah said. "I'll be up in a minute to help you change your clothes."

I climbed the stairs. There was time, before Aunt Sarah followed, to put Mother and Father's picture away. I was about to, but I paused, looking at them, and as I heard her step on the stairs, I decided to leave them where they were. No time like the present!

Aunt Sarah brought a candle and set it on the bedside table. It threw a soft glow directly onto the windowsill, touching the edge of the picture. She didn't glance that way. She was looking around the room. "It's awful hot up here!" It was true. The stale heat lingered in the corners of the room, like the remnants of a fever. "It must have been terrible during that hot weather. Why didn't you mention it, Harriet?"

She crossed the room and pushed the bureau aside with her hip. The murky mirror shuddered. She opened the door beyond, and after a moment cool air began to flow through my window, moving toward the next room.

Aunt Sarah paused in the doorway. "I'll move you over here tomorrow," she said. "That way you won't get the heat from the kitchen," She stood looking into that bare room for a moment. I leaned over and nudged the candle, so the warm glow lit Mother's face. Aunt Sarah turned and came toward me, the nightgown draped over her arm. I saw her see the picture.

She stood looking for a moment, and then she reached across the candle flame and picked up the picture. My heart beat harder: Mother and Aunt Sarah, face to face. She gazed and gazed, her eyes dark and wide.

"He *was* sick," she said finally, as if to herself. "I didn't realize . . . "

Then she seemed to remember that I was there. She looked down at me, huge in the twilit room, the photograph small in her hand. The candle lit the underside of it, lit the date in Mother's handwriting, lit the sudden glitter in Aunt Sarah's eyes.

"You'll want a frame for this," she said, "so you can have it on your table." Gently she propped the picture back in the window, a little farther over than I'd had it, so the candlelight fell only on Father's face, but never mind that for now.

"Stand up," she said, "and let me help you into your nightgown."

AUTHOR'S NOTE

This story was inspired by the real-life story of Helen Watts Chase, who was orphaned under different circumstances in 1889. Like Harry, Helen had lived with an indulgent mother and was left to the care of an aunt with different ideas about raising children. Her story is included in *Roxana's Children: The Biography of a Nineteenth-Century Vermont Family*, by Lynn A. Bonfield and Mary C. Morrison, published in 1995 by the University of Massachusetts Press.

Harry is not Helen but came into existence because of her.